A Quick Primer
on Wallowing in Despair:

Stories
by Steve Gergley

Praise for Steve Gergley

"*A Quick Primer on Wallowing in Despair* takes you through aliens, vanishing bodies and horseradish people and digs at what we keep buried inside of us. Steve Gergley is a master of combining seemingly disparate elements into a cohesive whole and accomplishes this brilliantly in his debut collection with its sentence level prose, individual story arcs and the way these different stories weave together into a single, almost absurdist yet also deeply human experience."
- Lucy Zhang, fiction editor of *Heavy Feather Review*

"A long-time fan of Steve Gergley's work, I'm always impressed by his range: Gergley's stories swing from gritty, sharp realism to speculative fantasy to wild, formal experimentalism. His desperado characters lurch through scenes both plausible and bizarre. Despite their desperate straits, they never lose hope. These stories are unpredictable, macabre, deadpan, both hilarious and harrowing, by an author who is entirely original."
- Kim Magowan, author of *How Far I've Come, The Light Source, Undoing.* Editor-in-Chief of Pithead Chapel

"In prose both breathless and frank, Gergley tells the stories of the pathetic and ridiculous with such empathy and honesty that one can't help but cheer for them, identify with them, and flip pages wondering what incredible thing will happen next. Each story in *A Quick Primer on Wallowing in Despair* is a surprise."
- Meagan Lucas, author of *Songbirds and Stray Dogs*, and Editor-in-Chief of *Reckon Review*

"Steve Gergley has managed to take my favorite kind of short stories and throw them into one fluid and fun collection. They are full of music and life. Each story has its own form of hidden bliss beneath the crushing blows that we are shackled to in real life. With each ebb and flow of despair, we are met with promise and adventure. Steve is a talented author with a flair for the abstract. Don't sleep on this book. It's something you're going to love."
– Mallory Smart, author of *The Only Living Girl in Chicago,* and Editor-in-Chief of *Maudlin House.*

Acknowledgments

Huge thanks to the editors of the journals in which these stories first appeared: "Lizzy from Lake Placid," "A Quick Primer on Wallowing in Despair," "Brain Debris vs. The Squid Aliens," "To You, in Another 31 Years," and "Who Cares What Psychiatrists Write on Walls?" in *Maudlin House*; "Red Means Go" in *Barren Magazine*; "Drilling" in *Drunk Monkeys*; "TooAfraidToAsk" and "Sexy Rexy's Homecoming Feast" in *X-R-A-Y Literary Magazine*; "You'll Never Leave" in *Ghost Parachute*; "There's a Crashing Plane Behind the Store" in *The Fiction Pool;* At Action Park" in *Atticus Review,* "Work-Life Balance" in *Déraciné Magazine*; "Monday Morning at the Office" forthcoming in *The Bookends Review*; "Auditing," "Medium," and "Why Can't I Fall Asleep?" in *Fictive Dream*; "Cryonics" in *Expat Press*; "Last Day of Fatassery" and "Apartment 4 1/2 B" in *Typishly Literary Magazine*; "The Guy Who Always Felt Like He Was About to Throw Up" in *Bending Genres*; "a few of my favorite words and why i like them," "Confession with Father Patrick," and "A Note About the Type" in *After the Pause*; "What is it?" in *Hobart*; "Some Things that Happened" in *BULL*; "I Found My Heel at the Foot of an Oak" in *Bridge Eight Literary Magazine*; "Manga," "Good Shit," and "Sunrise" collected as "Sunrise" in *Cleaver Magazine*; "J.B. in the Desert" in *Ligeia Magazine,* and "In the Garden of Earthly Delights" in *New World Writing*.

Table of Contents

Lizzy from Lake Placid

The day after my thirty-fourth birthday, I had a dream about Lana Del Rey. In the dream me and Lana were sitting on a California beach at midnight, smoking weed while the moon glinted above like a silver coin on a summer sidewalk. Waking up I realized that the dream had probably just been a side-effect of me listening to "High by the Beach" on repeat while getting drunk on Merlot with my mom last night, but then I remembered my best friend Lizzy G from middle school, and I realized that she and Lana were the same person. Checking Lana's bio on Wikipedia I confirmed my theory: both women shared the given name Elizabeth; both were former church singers who grew up in my hometown of Lake Placid; both had trouble with booze starting in middle school; both had a mother who taught at the local high school. Reading all that, I had no doubt: my best friend from middle school had gone on to become my favorite singer in the world.

With this in mind I had to go and see her. Even though we hadn't talked since her parents had shipped her off to a Connecticut catholic school when we were fifteen, I knew she'd remember her girl Nikki. So I fired up Google and checked her touring schedule. She was in Atlanta tonight, but in three days she'd be performing at Roseland Ballroom in NYC, a little less than an hour and a half from where I was sitting right now, in my house in Topine, NY. And since I didn't have to be back at work until Sunday morning, two days after the concert, the timing worked out perfectly. The only problem was getting there. Because of my DUI back in March, my driver's license had been suspended. And I knew Mom would never drive me there because she was still pissed at me for moving back in with her without asking after I broke up with Tyler last month. So for the next hour I lay in bed, finished off the last half-bottle of Merlot left over from last night, and thought about what to do. A few minutes after that, it came to me.

By noon I was pedaling my bike down Black Cherry Road, making my way to the bus station. The cool summer wind cut past my cheeks, and the soft gold light of the sun warmed the backs of my hands. Then, as I sliced past Geno's Second, the pizza place where Mom and I worked as waitresses, I turned my head and hid my face behind my hand. Mom was working the lunch shift all day today, so the last thing I needed was for her to see me riding past the restaurant on my bike, half-drunk and without a helmet. This was exactly the kind of stupid stuff she used to do back when I was a kid, but of course whenever I do it, it's wrong. For as long as I could remember, she'd been the kind of mom who would down a glass of wine just before lecturing me about the evils of alcohol. As a drinking buddy she's a lot of fun, but as a parent she's a complete mess.

Ten minutes later I realized I hadn't yet bought a ticket to Lana's show. So I turned into a quiet housing development full of towering sugar maples and pastel-colored colonials. From here I took out my phone, slowed to a leisurely coast, and tried to order my ticket to Lana's show. Just then my bike smashed into something big and my phone jumped out of my hand. I flew over my handlebars, tumbled across the trunk of a car, and pancaked onto the pavement. After this I felt very tired, and my knees and elbows started to hurt a lot, so I closed my eyes and relaxed. The pain swept over me in little rhythmic splashes.

I must've fallen asleep for a while, because the next time I opened my eyes, the parked car I'd run into had been moved into a nearby driveway. In its place stood a college-age girl with a phone pressed to her ear. She was skinny and tall and had a long brown ponytail and square glasses.

"Please don't call my mother," I said to the girl. "She'll kick me out again if she finds out about this."

"I'm not calling your mother, I'm calling an ambulance."

"Don't call them either."

"But I have to. You're hurt."

"It's fine," I said, pressing my aching palms into the pavement and pushing myself up into a sit. "I'm okay. I swear."

The girl stared at me for another long moment and then looked around the development.

Following her gaze I saw an old man sitting in a rocking chair on his porch next door, but he wasn't watching us. His head was thrown back to the sky in sleep or death or something else. Other than that, the street was empty.

The girl turned back to me.

"But your elbows and knees are all cut up."

"Okay, okay. You drive a hard bargain, sister," I said, feeling dizzy and drunk. "If you promise to not tell anyone about this, I won't tell anyone either. It'll be a secret between girls."

"I don't know."

I stood up to show her that everything was fine. My knees and elbows stung a lot, and I was pretty shaky on my feet, but other than that everything seemed okay.

"I'm fine, I swear," I said. Now I remembered my dream from last night and the fact that Lana was my old best friend. With that in mind this whole situation suddenly seemed very silly and unreal, so I said the first thing that came into my head. "By the way, do you have any weed?"

#

For the next few minutes the girl helped me clean my cuts. Her name was Kristin. After this I took a bath in her house and she let me use some of her mom's scented bath oils. Laying in the hot water, I breathed wet air spiked with chamomile and lavender. When I came out of the bath she said her parents were out of town for the week so we didn't have to worry about them coming home and asking questions. Then she offered me some wine. She didn't have the weed I'd asked for, but apparently her mom had some Pinot noir in the basement, so once that was in hand we trudged into the backyard and opened the bottle. From the weariness in her face I could tell she'd been waiting all morning for an excuse to start drinking. I knew that look all too well. I saw it staring back at me every time I looked in the mirror these days.

At the back of her property was a creek. In front of the creek was an old Weber grill and a square of bricks set into the grass. The square was no more than fifteen or twenty feet wide, and on the far side of the square sat a stone staircase that went straight down into the creek. That was something I'd never seen before.

For the next hour we sat by the creek and drank the wine. While we drank, Kristin told me about herself. She was a freshman over at Topine Community College, but she wasn't doing so great and was thinking about taking a year off. I told her that if she was even thinking that, then she'd already made the decision in her head, so it was probably best to just drop out already and move on. As I spoke, I realized this was something my mom would've told me in the same situation. I didn't like that. I didn't want to be a Negative Nancy like her, always tearing people down. After that Kristin went quiet for a while. In this quiet I told her that my old best friend from middle school was Lana Del Rey, but she was doubtful about this. Even after I presented all my evidence she still didn't believe me. She told me the probability was very low that my friend and Lana were the same person. To humor her I looked up at the sky and pretended to think hard about what she had said. But instead I imagined what it would feel like to walk down those stairs into the creek and to float away forever. That seemed like the best course of action at this point in my life. But I didn't do that. Instead I reached for the bottle and asked Kristin if she was similar to her mom in any way.

"Not really," she said. "I'm much more like my dad I think."

It was a good day. She was an easy girl to like.

Red Means Go

Adam sat beside Cass in a silver Toyota in the back of the CVS parking lot, his internal organs sheathed in frost, his thin body sore and shivering, his nose like a gross faucet left open oozing slick goop around cracked lips, his eyes leaking forever with the kind of acid tears that cook the eyeballs like poached eggs. The car was off because Adam had turned it off a while ago because he had started to get paranoid that the two workers inside the CVS would somehow see the gray line of exhaust rising from the running car and in seeing this they would get suspicious and would instantly know what he and Cass were planning to do and then they would call the cops on them and he'd have to endure the hell of spending the night in jail without having had a taste in almost twenty-four hours but no that wasn't right because by then it'd be longer than that and Christ Jesus he didn't even want to think about that so he looked down at his trembling right hand and saw the .357 snub nose in his hand and felt its satisfying weight in his hand and he remembered the two bullets he had loaded in it back at Young Jim's place and he checked the safety and made sure for the eight hundredth time tonight that the little lever was snapped into the safe position instead of the fire position and in doing this he realized that maybe it wasn't the job he was worried about but instead maybe he was just paranoid and anxious and pissed off at himself for being so stupid last night and for blowing through the stuff he'd been saving for the morning to keep away the sick even though he couldn't even remember the hit which was a goddamn shame and a crime but maybe the job wouldn't be too bad after all as long as he did it exactly how Young Jim had told him to do it so he started to go over the plan one more time in his head to make sure he had it straight. Okay. Reciting the steps in his head, Adam started to imagine how things would unfold eleven minutes from now when he would finally climb back into the world and walk across the dark parking lot with the snub nose in his pocket but then Cass said something for the first time in forever and he lost his train of thought and from here he turned to her in anger even though he couldn't see her very well with her face hidden in the dark and the haze of her cigarette smoke but then she leaned back in her seat and the orange glow of a nearby streetlight threw some light on her hair and the side of her face and looking there he saw that her hair was as thin and dry as parched scrub grass and her skin hung loose from the jagged knives of her cheekbones and angular chin and in this moment she looked as horrible as an Egyptian mummy come to life like that bald guy in that movie Adam used to love back in middle school ten thousand years ago and in remembering this Adam's anger suddenly vanished because it killed him to see her like this, this girl he sometimes loved and couldn't live without but at other times hated for being nothing more than another greedy vein to feed, and then she turned her face into the orange light and his gaze met hers for the first time in what seemed like days and her eyes looked like dead marbles without anything inside, no life, no energy, just hunger and sadness and desperation, so he quickly looked away and squeezed the grip of the snub nose and spoke quietly but forcefully to her.

"Christ, can you please shut up for a second please, babe? I got to run through this shit again so I don't screw it up because that's the last goddamn thing we need. So please, let's just shut up for a second so I can think through it again."

"You thinking. That's a new one. Good luck with that." She blew a hot exhale of cigarette smoke out her window she had opened by a third.

At this he ignored her and thought hard to remember the plan Young Jim had told him earlier in the day: go into the CVS ten minutes before close, hang out by the milk cooler, wait for the guy wearing the tie to take the cash drawers up into the office, swing behind the counter and catch the door before it closes, show him the gun and tell him to empty the safe into a—

"You know, you really got to work on that mouth of yours, baby. Everything is shut up this, goddamn that. That's no way to talk to people. You don't hear Tommy talking that way to people."

Hearing her again he pressed his burning eyes closed and tried to keep Young Jim's words straight in his head, but the reedy scratch of her voice and the mention of that name shattered them apart and all the disparate pieces fell to the floor in his brain and jumbled up in the wrong order.

"Can you just be quiet for two goddamn seconds please, babe? Christ." He squeezed the grip of the snub nose and folded his fingers away from the trigger as a few cups of chilled sweat beaded up on his hot skin and crawled down his face. Moments later a tectonic rumble of nausea rolled through his stomach and brought his forehead down against the sticky rubber of the steering wheel. Soon the nausea passed and he sat up and wiped the sweat from his eyes with shaking fingers. Seven minutes. "Goddamn Tommy. If I was you I wouldn't put too much faith into anything Tommy says. You don't know him like I do. I've been dealing with his psycho manipulator bullshit for twenty years. Guy's nothing but a lying junkie thief and once we're done with this job, we're done with him for good, got that? We're never going to get clean if we keep bumming around in that goddamn apartment with that goddamn parasite."

Cass scoffed and looked away and flipped her stringy hair at him and blew some smoke out her window and shrugged.

"Whatever you say, baby. He's your cousin. All I'm saying is that at least Tommy has a job. At least Tommy has his own place and a bed to sleep in at night. When was the last time you got any of that for us?" She lifted her shriveled, old-woman hand to the top of her open window and dropped the cigarette outside.

Three minutes. He checked the safety one last time and stuck the snub nose in his pocket and zipped up the long, baggy sweatshirt he'd brought to hide the bulge in his pocket.

"Whatever. All I know is that if it wasn't for that asshole, I wouldn't even have gotten started on any of this—" he started to say, but he stopped himself there and let his words dissolve in the air because yes it was true that Tommy was the person he had smoked his first joint with and yes Tommy was the person who had first introduced him to heroin and had showed him how to shoot up ("When shooting heroin, red means go . . . ") and yes he hated Tommy for those reasons and a hundred others, but he hated Tommy more so for the fact that the man pushed off daily but still somehow managed to hold on to all the essential pieces of himself while everyone around him had been eaten alive by the dope and had been shat out into the inescapable black hole of lying and stealing and sickness and desperation and debasement and shame that was Adam's life right now. But Adam knew he didn't have time to be thinking about any of this, so he banished these thoughts from his head and turned to Cass and reminded her one last time about her end of the plan.

"Okay babe, do you remember what you need to do?

All you have to do is wait FIVE minutes from when I get out of the car, and then you just have to BACK it into a space in front of the store and leave the doors unlocked and the engine running," Adam said. His face felt like a cheap rubber mask glued to his skull. As he talked, Cass stared at her hands in her lap and nodded to the cadence of something other than his words. "Okay? And don't worry about the guys inside. Young Jim used to work there and he promised me they're not going to do anything. He said they get fired if they try to do anything, so we don't have to worry okay?"

Cass nodded and gave an affirmative grunt in response. One minute.

"Okay." He snapped off his seatbelt and let it whip against the door on his left. "Last one babe, and then we're done with this shit for good. Okay? Once we have this dough we'll pay off that asshole Tommy and then we'll cop enough stuff to keep away the sick and then we're done. No more. Then it's off to that place down in Jersey where they got that miracle drug that'll help us get clean. That's the one my brother was telling us about, remember? And if dumbass Leo can do it, anyone can. And then once we're clean we'll get a place of our own, and everything will be beautiful. I've still got a year left on my forklift license, so I shouldn't have a problem finding a job down there. And once we're all set up I'll buy you one of those fancy-ass electric keyboards so you can play piano whenever you want. It's going to be beautiful babe, I promise. We're almost there, okay? Just back her into a spot in front of the store and leave the engine running."

Zero minutes and she was still staring at her hands in her lap and her face was hidden by her hair that looked like dry hay. Now he reached out with his trembling hand and tried to hold hers for a moment, but just before his fingers touched her skin, she nodded again and spoke.

"Okay baby," she said in a quiet voice. "Whatever you say."

From here a pair of headlights shined in his eyes and splattered the interior of the car with a momentary flash of white light. Following this he looked at the clock and saw that he was two minutes late, so he huffed out a hard exhale and clicked the door open. A cool breeze kissed the side of his sweaty neck. Not wanting to jinx the job by leaving on crappy terms, he told her he loved her. It felt good to say this because for the first time in a very long while, he meant it. So on this note he climbed out of the car and closed the door softly, the way he assumed a normal person would close the door when making a late-night stop at CVS.

#

For a minute after she heard the thunk of the car door closing, Cass sat with her eyes closed in the warmth and quiet of the empty car. Through the open window at her right she heard the sticky chirping of summer bugs, the whirring screech of a distant car, and the rhythmic thump of a blasting radio, but she wasn't paying attention to these sounds or any others outside her head. No, the only sound Cass cared about in that moment was the alluring song of the two baggies of dope Tommy had given her this morning after their usual covert fuck, the silent voice of the dope sounding more beautiful to her than the melodies of Clair de Lune or Satie's Gymnopédies or Beethoven's Waltz in E flat major or any of the other pieces she used to play for her mom and Gramma April at her piano recitals back in the stone age of her childhood. But as much as she wanted to dump out her purse and get the bags and find the nearest public bathroom to have a taste right now, she knew she couldn't use them just yet. First she had to wait for her dumbass, wannabe criminal boyfriend to head into the CVS he thought he was going to knock over. Only then would she finally have the time she needed to have another taste without him finding out. Because if he saw that she had extra dope she wasn't sharing with him, he'd instantly know she'd gotten it from Tommy, and that they were fucking behind his back. And then he'd go nuts, like usual. From there he'd probably drive over to Tommy's place like a crazy person and force Tommy to kill him. And then they'd all be screwed. So as much as her tired brain and muddy veins ached for a taste, her mind was clear enough to know that she needed to wait. So she leaned back in her seat and chewed her gnarled lip and watched as Adam tripped over the curb on his way into the CVS.

Three seconds after Adam entered the store, Cass clambered over the center column and slid into the driver's seat. Now her body moved on its own: finger pressed ignition button, foot stomped brake pedal, palm cupped stick-shift, hand gripped steering wheel. Soon the car was moving, gliding across the dark parking lot, turning onto Pinehill Road, and speeding toward the twenty-four-hour Shoprite just down the street. From here her heart smashed and her mouth watered just thinking about the safety and seclusion of that public bathroom, that place where she would finally be alone once again with that magic dust that was the only force powerful enough to incinerate the metric tons of garbage that had been stacked in her brain for years by her piece- of-shit step-father and his drunken visits to her room each night after bedtime, that reeking landfill of pain and disassociation that for so long she had tried to bury under grassy mounds of politeness and charity and the beauty of her music, but of course it came back, it always did, even on days like today when Tommy woke her up for their secret morning fuck while that dummy Adam was still passed out, even then she still sometimes felt the paralyzing electric twinge of it crackling down her spine, but she didn't have to worry about that right now because soon she'd be free of it once again, the dope granting her the greatest gift anything had ever given her, the gift of forgetting, of living a life where those things never happened to her, and now here it was, the mouth of the parking lot she'd been looking for, and so the dark wall of trees parted and the black tongue of blacktop rolled out to meet her and she turned into the lot and parked crooked in a space near the door and then she was out in the warm dark and inside the cool store and her shoes were silent on the shiny floor and her eyes felt large in her head and there were giant pallets of plastic-wrapped food at the end of every aisle and she couldn't stop smiling but it didn't matter because all the workers were scruffy teenagers with tufts of patchy facial hair and white-wired headphones in their ears and eyes bloodshot from the weed they probably smoked during the drive into work and then an instant later she was there at the ladies room and then inside and a quick bend and peek at the stalls showed that she was alone so she walked back to the bathroom door and locked it and then she went into the spacious handicapped stall at the end and suddenly everything was already set and the needle was in her hand and she felt the sharp little bite of steel breaking skin and then she pulled the plunger back and watched the feathery plume of red swirl and rise ("Red means go . . . ") and then pressing down with her thumb her eyes rolled in her skull like billiard balls on felt and gold light filled her body and three years passed and her head fell forever down toward her knees but it never quite got there and an unlit cigarette hung loosely from her lips, the paper sticking to her dry lips as a shining line of drool touched the floor and the universe outside her head dissolved away into nothing and she felt perfectly at peace.

#

Back in the CVS, Adam stood in front of the milk cooler as a hurricane of nausea swirled in his stomach and a waterfall of icy sweat ran down his boiling face. Staring through the foggy glass, he waited for the worker in the nice white shirt and cool blue tie to take the registers up to the office so he could catch the door and put the money in a bag and then show the guy the gun and get him to open the safe but no that wasn't right he'd have to show him the gun first and then the guy would open the safe and put the money in a bag and yes that was the right order but just as soon as he had that straight some muscles in his stomach tightened up and clenched on their own until they were stone hard and burning hot and because of this he could barely expand his chest far enough to slurp the tiniest breath so he bent over and pressed his wet hands against his knees for support and while in this position he was strangled with the terrible fear that he was having a heart attack right here in this stupid little store with a gun in his pocket but then his stomach muscles relaxed and he gulped a heaving breath and leaned a heavy hand against the side of the cooler and when he looked up a minute later he saw that the two CVS workers were suddenly standing right beside him, asking him if he was okay. Still not sure whether he was having a heart attack or not, Adam suddenly didn't care about what Young Jim had said and now he just wanted to get the goddamn money so he could get the hell out of here and get back to Young Jim's place and have a goddamn taste to get rid of this goddamn sick so he reached into his pocket and took out the snub nose and pointed it at the guy with the white shirt and blue tie and because he couldn't hear his own voice over his heartbeat smashing in his ears, Adam shouted at the guy to get behind the counter and to empty the registers into a bag. Then, as the guy with the blue tie held up his hands and walked behind the counter, Adam remembered about the safety that was still on so he turned the

snub nose on its side and with his left hand snapped the little
lever into the fire position and then pointed it back at the guy
with the blue tie but as he did this the gun almost slipped from
his sweat-slick fingers so he clenched his hand tight to stop it from
falling and suddenly he heard a loud crack and felt a hard jolt
scream up his arm and in an instant the guy in the blue tie was
gone and the place smelled like smoke so Adam jogged to the
edge of the counter and looked over it to see what had happened
and looking there he saw that the guy in the white shirt and blue
tie was crumpled on the ground and his shirt was soaked in red
and seeing this redness Adam turned around and started running
toward the front door where Cass would be waiting with the car
but before he got there he felt another churn of magma in his
stomach and he remembered the sick and how desperately he
needed a taste so he turned back to the other worker who had
been standing next to the milk cooler with his hands up and his
eyes closed and he shoved the snub nose into the worker's back
and said some words he hoped were a command for the guy to
stay still and then he reached into the guy's back pocket and took
the guy's wallet and opened it and took out the two twenty dollar
bills that were in there and then he dropped the wallet on the
ground and started for the front door but stopped a second later
because he knew forty bucks would never be enough for both
him and Cass and so without a moment of hesitation he turned
around again and this time he ran for the back door instead of
the front. Moments later he was at the back door and then
through it and stumbling into the storeroom but now there was a
horrible screeching noise of some alarm he had tripped and with
feet smacking on concrete he scrambled to another door with
red words printed across the push- bar and he pressed the bar in
but it didn't move so he took out the gun and looked for a lock
to aim it at like people do in the movies but he didn't see one
and with the alarm screeching in his ears and his heart pounding
in his mouth he couldn't hear or think so he started kicking the
push- bar with all his strength, the shocks of each impact
resonating in his knee, and after five or six kicks the door scraped
open an inch and smelling freedom he threw his shoulder into it
and burst through into a barren parking lot bathed in the orange
light of some spotlight overhead and from here he streaked past
a loading dock and a rusty green dumpster and moments later he
made the woods behind the CVS and once there he started to

climb back into his skin and in doing so he suddenly remembered about the snub nose in his hand so he stopped running and he bent down and dug a little hole in the cool dirt and he put the snub nose in the hole and pressed the dirt back on top and stomped the dirt a few times and threw some leaves on top of the dirt. Four seconds later he was up and running again and yes he was lost in the woods right now and yes he felt like radioactive feces right now but soon he would be back at Young Jim's place and soon the needle would be in his arm once again and seconds after that he wouldn't remember any of this, not Cass or the guy in the blue tie or the pipe-dream future of Jersey, and in thinking about this he knew everything would be okay again soon because with the dope in his veins and the sick far away, there was no such thing as tomorrow.

STEVE GERGLEY

A Quick Primer on Wallowing in Despair
Wallow on, dudes!
Posted by: C. J. Richardson - 55 minutes ago

So you're depressed. Your life is a failure. Every dream and aspiration you've ever had is gone and out of reach. Even your back-up plans, the ones your parents always told you to have just in case, the ones you kept hidden in the back of your mind and hoped you'd never have to turn to, those ones have gone kaput, too. Now you've got nothing. No one. Well, not no one, because if you say you have no one at all in your life, like zero people, that would be a lie. But what you really mean is that you have no one who matters. So you feel like shit. Garbage.

Human waste. A regurgitated Taco Bell value meal that's been stomped into the muddy cracks in the pavement outside the city dump. You're tired, weak, apathetic. Most mornings you don't have the strength/energy/desire to peel the covers off your disgusting, bloated body that not even a blind, horny, seventeen-year-old Chihuahua would want to hump. So you stay in bed. You wallow. You marinate in your despair and ask the ceiling what you did wrong to end up as a single, overweight, twenty-eight-year-old failure with bad skin who is back home living with her parents. We get it. We've been there. The good news is we can help. Believe it or not, we here at Procrastination Station have a good amount of experience with the whole, wallowing in despair thing. So, dear procrastinator, if you want to learn more about getting through this difficult time in your pathetic life, be sure to read our three quick tips below!

Quick Tip #1: When wallowing in despair, time is the biggest obstacle you're going to have to overcome each day. For you, lying in bed, staring up at the dimpled ceiling, practicing your vocal fry technique (look it up), time will seem to slow down to the speed at which an ant walks across the street. Actually, that might be a little fast. Either way, time is a problem because of your thoughts. Contrary to popular belief, when wallowing in despair, you're actually going to be spending most of your time wide awake and bored. And during these periods, thinking is just about the only thing you'll have at your disposal to stave off your boredom. (Because I mean, let's be real. It's not like you're going to get up to turn on the TV. That would require energy, motivation, strength—you know, all that stuff you don't have left in the useless, hollowed-out skinbag that is your body.) That being said, you don't want to be thinking. That's bad. Because the more you think, the more you're going to fixate on the humiliating, irreversible mistakes you've made in your wasted life. Mistakes like the time you turned down that staff writer job at The Topine Gazette because you thought your hometown newspaper was below you. Or the day you suspected your boyfriend of three years of having an emotional affair with one of his female co-workers and hacked into his phone to find proof but instead discovered that it really was his ex-girlfriend's mom who had texted him. And as weird and not normal as that may be, you don't want to be thinking about that right now. So, to combat this, we suggest making mental lists. Top ten lists work nicely: Top Ten Favorite Movies, Top Ten Favorite Actresses, Top Ten Best Albums of the 2010s, and so on. These will redirect your thoughts to subjects that naturally give you pleasure, while at the same time bringing you ever closer to the wonderful bliss of your next nap. And since these lists are so common on the internet (Procrastination Station has an entire page dedicated to nothing but these kinds of lists, just sayin'), you can probably think up a half dozen ideas without much effort.

Quick Tip #2: Food is the second pitfall to watch out for when wallowing in despair. Since you don't have the energy or desire to get out of bed, you're probably going to be skipping a meal or two. This is not a good idea. Because when you skip meals to focus on your wallowing, you're going to become very hungry later in the day. And this hunger, coupled with your lowered impulse control and apathy toward your personal wellbeing, can lead to bingeing. So watch out! You wouldn't believe how quickly your one a.m. trudge to the kitchen for a cheese sandwich can balloon into a ninety-minute chomp-fest starring a half pound of Boar's Head turkey breast, a brick of cheddar cheese, half a bag of fun-size Mounds candy bars left over from Halloween, a tub of mint chocolate chip ice cream drowned in half a bottle of chocolate syrup, and a box of frozen sausage links that fell out of the freezer when you opened the door. This is especially dangerous because at first, bingeing can be a very effective escape from the pain of your worthless existence. But if allowed to continue, it can lead to severe bloating, vicious stomach aches, high-pressure gas build-up that is so extreme you cannot sit down for hours, and other health risks in both the near and distant future. So remember: you might be utterly alone in this world, completely unworthy of being loved by another human being, but with three balanced, nutritious meals each day, you've got friends at your side!

Quick Tip #3: Lastly, the most important thing to stay away from over the course of your wallowing, is social media. In your boredom, you may be tempted to use social media for a number of reasons: pretending the cute, playful tweets Ryan Reynolds sends to Blake Lively are actually intended for you; looking up your ex-boyfriend and comparing the physical attractiveness of his wife to the version of yourself just before he broke up with you, thereby making yourself feel worse for the sole purpose of experiencing any emotion at all. But as tempting as these activities may be, they are not a productive use of your interminable free time. As you probably already know, social media is not a realistic representation of a person's life.

It's more of an idealized, public-facing facade carefully constructed to portray the individual in the best possible light. Think of it as a family photo album: inside, the pages are filled with beautiful shots of graduations, birthdays, shiny new cars, and smiling faces, but nowhere is there a photo of the father's sudden heart attack, the married couple screaming at each other over who's turn it is to take out the garbage, or the twelve-year-old girl slicing small cuts into the back of her heel with the spare razorblade from her father's shaving kit. And if you start ingesting the polished, distorted version of someone else's reality, you're only going to feel worse about your own pitiful life in comparison. So just stay away. If you start to feel tempted, ask yourself this: when was the last time someone live-tweeted her father's double-bypass heart surgery?

So those are our three tips. If you follow these, dear procrastinator, you'll be well on your way to safely navigating this trying time in your life. But whatever happens, remember this: despite what your brain is telling you right now, there's always the small possibility that the world is actually not a terrible, reeking cesspool of pain, suffering, loneliness, and despair. And who knows? Maybe someday you'll find some evidence to support that theory. But until then, good luck, stay safe, and happy wallowing!

Brain Debris vs. The Squid Aliens

Dawn had only been in Brain Debris for six months, but already her headbanging was legendary. Sure, all the bands in the New York death metal scene headbanged while ripping through their songs in the local clubs—it was one of the treasured traditions of the genre after all, alongside extra-large black t-shirts and devil-horned fists punching the sweat-thickened air—but Dawn's headbanging was different. It was more ferocious, more animalistic, and wilder than any of the other musicians in the scene. While other guitarists waited until the verse to nod and to sway and to swirl their messy ropes of dry, kinky, waist-length hair, Dawn started headbanging the moment each song began. And unlike the other guitarists she knew, Dawn didn't stop headbanging to play the difficult parts. Instead, whenever the band transitioned into the bridge and Peer started playing the support riff for her solo, Dawn braced her Ibanez against her left thigh and thrashed with wild abandon while her fingers raced up and down the fretboard, sliding, tapping, hammering-on, pulling-off, and squeezing out the piggish squeal of an occasional pinch harmonic.

And it was here, on a chilly Thursday night in March, while Dawn and the rest of Brain Debris stood in the back corner of The Luna Cafe and played, "Rotting Dreamscapes," the second song off their self-titled EP, that Dawn first felt the sawing at the back of her head. The feeling wasn't as powerful as the guttural roars of Ray's vocals, the explosive blast beats of Tony's drums, or the sawtooth buzz of Peer's rhythm guitar, but still she felt it amidst the chaos of the entire song, as if a surgeon was trying to cut through the back of her skull with a white-hot scalpel of light. Six times she felt the sharp, searing slice of this strange sensation, and six times she thrashed her head with such force that the sensation disappeared momentarily, before returning seconds later.

By the end of the next song, the sensation went away for good. Here Dawn parted the curtain of frizzy blonde hair hanging in front of her face and scanned the crowd for her girlfriend, Heather. Dawn and Heather had been together for almost three months, and to Dawn's very pleasant surprise, she now liked Heather even more than she had when they first started messaging each other on Tinder back in December. Usually things moved in the opposite direction: the better Dawn got to know someone, the less she liked them. There were just too many irregularities about Dawn that other people couldn't understand: her clothes, her musical tastes, her anger issues (that were mostly in the past), her lifestyle of playing guitar in metal and hardcore bands. But Heather was different from everyone else in Dawn's life. Heather was on the autism spectrum, a music lover like herself, and the most accepting person Dawn had ever met. Unlike everyone outside the scene, Heather didn't cringe or laugh or cower away in fear when Dawn said she loved metal and hardcore and that she played guitar in a band called Brain Debris. Instead, Heather looked at Dawn with her beautiful, silver-blue eyes, brushed a blade of long brown hair behind her ear, and asked Dawn to play something. This happened during Dawn and Heather's third date, while they watched TV in Peer's basement, a half-finished space that doubled as Dawn's apartment and the band's practice room. At the time, Dawn had just finished writing, "Chasms of Consciousness," a thirteen-minute epic for Brain Debris' upcoming full- length album, so as a joke, Dawn told Heather about it. But since Heather didn't understand sarcasm, she asked Dawn to play the song for her. Shocked, intrigued, and more than a little bit flattered, Dawn nodded and played the entire song. When it was over, Heather gaped at Dawn with childlike awe and said, I don't really understand a lot of what you were doing just now, but that was the most badass thing I've ever heard. Since then, Dawn felt a warm, giddy, fluttery feeling in her stomach each time she looked at Heather. And that was something she had never experienced before.

But when Dawn finally found Heather standing among the sparse crowd of twenty or thirty people in the back room of The Luna Cafe, Heather didn't wink or wave or even look at her. Instead, she stared at the wall to Dawn's right and pressed her hands to the back of her head in the exact place where Dawn had felt that weird sawing sensation for the last two songs. Dawn waved and called out Heather's name, but Heather ignored her. Then Dawn looked at the rest of the crowd and noticed that they were doing the same thing. Turning around, she looked at Tony and Ray and Peer. They too stared at the wall while their hands cupped the backs of their heads like pieces of precious fruit.

Moments later the wall to Dawn's right dissolved in a flash of blinding light. A golden haze leaked in through the hole in the wall. Squinting through the haze, Dawn looked around the room and saw four squid-like creatures flying in the air near the ceiling. The creatures flew in smooth, easy circles, as if they were swimming through still water. The creatures' bodies were completely transparent, like the strange fish that lived near thermal vents in the lightless depths of the ocean, and the only time Dawn could see them was when they passed through a thick patch of the golden haze. Each time they did, Dawn saw tiny beams of gold light stretch between the squid creatures' undulating tentacles and the backs of the heads of every person in the room. Everyone except her.

To prevent the squid creatures from discovering that she was not hypnotized, Dawn placed her hands on the back of her head like everyone else. Soon a white craft shaped like a giant breath mint appeared next to the hole in the wall. Hovering soundlessly just above the ground, the craft looked to be a little bit smaller than Dawn's crappy old Toyota Camry.

Moments later the side of the craft opened, revealing a silky black void within.

The squid creatures emitted a quiet, pleasing hum and glowed with gold light. In a single synchronized movement, everyone in the crowd started walking toward the hovering craft. With her heart thudding in her chest and her breath catching in her throat, Dawn lowered her hands from her head and ran to Heather. But Dawn's Ibanez was still plugged into her amp, so before she reached Heather, her guitar cable pulled taut and jangled the strings of her guitar. A sharp jolt of dissonant noise clanged through the room. The squid creatures shrieked in what sounded like pain, and the hypnotized crowd, including Heather, stopped marching and pressed their hands to their ears.

Seeing this, Dawn knew what she had to do. So she walked back to the corner of the room, looked at her hypnotized bandmates, and started playing the intro to her thirteen-minute epic, "Chasms of Consciousness." As she thrashed her body in a frenzy and tore through sixteenth-note runs and palm-muted open-e chugs, scalpels of light began sawing at her head, her wrists, the fingers of her left hand. She didn't care. She simply played faster, headbanged harder.

Tony was the first member of Brain Debris to escape from the squid creatures' mind control. Halfway through the first verse, his drums entered the song. Here Dawn felt the concussive force of his double bass slamming against the backs of her legs. Peer's rhythm guitar woke up next. It lent force and body to Dawn's riffs; it elevated her leads atop a thick slab of churning sludge. Ray's bass and vocals came in last, which was not surprising since he had always been a little slow on the uptake, but Dawn didn't fault him for that. The band had been rehearsing the song for over two months, and Dawn still hadn't written any lyrics for it. It didn't matter. Ray roared his own lyrics with the fury of a demonic beast baking in the fires of hell.

Though the squid creatures seemed to be getting weaker and swimming slower the longer the song continued, the scalpels of light sawing at Dawn's body burned hotter than before, and bit deeply into her flesh. By the time Peer started playing the support riff for Dawn's solo, her black hoodie was damp with blood.

Then, as Dawn launched into her solo with a sweep-picked arpeggio starting at the fifteenth fret of the second string, the squid creatures glowed brighter than ever before and swam furiously in a tight circle. From behind the veil of her swinging hair, Dawn saw the thin filaments of light disconnect from the heads of everyone in the crowd. Dawn felt a giddy flutter in her chest. She looked at Heather and smiled. But then the squid creatures and the hovering craft exploded into glittering dust and a thick beam of gold light flashed across the room. The beam struck Dawn in the center of the chest. Her body roared in pain. The floor flew up under her chin. The last note of her final solo rang into silence. Dawn didn't understand much of anything that happened next, but she recognized the face hovering above her as the world went dark: the silver-blue eyes, the long brown hair, the warm lips pressed against her own.

Drilling

On the ceiling, Patrick Star runs the rolling hills of Jellyfish Fields, a bamboo jellyfishing net grasped firmly in his fingerless fist. Below, Kyoko K climbs into the scrunching leather dental chair and opens wide.

At twenty-seven, K is nearly two decades older than the rest of Dr. Fred's regular patients, but since Topine Family Dental is the only dental practice in town that accepts her crappy health insurance, she's here in this empty office tonight, staring at the Spongebob stickers on the walls, waiting for Dr. Fred to start drilling the cavity in her bottom right molar.

"Hello again, Mrs. K," Dr. Fred says, towering over K like a skyscraper. "So it's just the one filling tonight? You're sure I can't interest you in a two-for-one deal? You are our last customer for the night."

Without giving K a chance to answer, Dr. Fred laughs a booming laugh and pulls up a stool. As he snaps on a pair of latex gloves, a thirty-year-old woman in turquoise scrubs enters the room and delivers a tray of glinting steel dental tools and a small syringe.

"You're the best, Janny-poo," Dr. Fred says, winking at the woman. The woman gives him a mischievous smile and runs her hand along his shoulders and leaves the room. Following the woman's exit, the thick, fruity smell of strawberry perfume hangs in the air.

Dr. Fred breathes a contented sigh and picks up the syringe. As he leans over K's open mouth, his cheeks flush red; his eyes go glazed and watery; his lips behind his clear face shield curl into a sloppy grin. Though it worries K to see her dentist devolve into something resembling a drunken frat boy just before drilling into her teeth, she tells herself it's nothing and lets it go. After moving into a new house with her husband Nick last month and starting a part-time job working the cash register at the Value King supermarket down the street, the last thing K needs right now is more stress.

"Just a little pinch to numb the pain," Dr. Fred says, raising the syringe.

Moments before K feels the bite of the needle, Dr. Fred turns his head and looks at something in the hallway. Worried,

K follows his gaze and sees the woman in the turquoise scrubs bent over in front of a supply closet, her rear end sticking out into the hallway. As if sensing their eyes on her, the woman looks over her shoulder, raises her eyebrows at Dr. Fred, and licks her lips.

Dr. Fred groans softly and gives K the shot of lidocaine. But with his gaze still fixed on the woman in the hallway, he misses K's gums and jams the syringe into the side of her tongue instead.

"Mmmmmm," K says, moaning in pain. She presses her eyes closed and crushes the dental chair's armrests. Hot tears slide down her cheeks and leak into her ears.

"Yup, ah, that's perfect, just like that," Dr. Fred says, his voice soft and breathy and distant.

With her tongue roaring in pain and her blood beating in her ears, K raises her right leg and slams her heel against the footrest of the dental chair. The loud metallic clang jolts Dr. Fred from his reverie and he calmly removes the syringe from K's mouth.

"Okay, so while we wait for the lidocaine to take effect, we'll get everything else ready to go," Dr. Fred says, finally tearing his gaze from the woman in the turquoise scrubs. Then he slides his stool in front of the computer behind K and starts typing.

K spits a rope of blood into the rinsing bowl and groans in pain. Despite the presence of the lidocaine, the sharp, throbbing pain in her tongue gets more intense by the minute. Then, as she turns around and tries to get Dr. Fred's attention to tell him about this pain, she catches a glimpse of the woman in the hallway. The woman is still rummaging through the supply closet just as before, but now the top of her turquoise scrubs is gone, and her black bra is in full view of anyone who might walk into the office. Threaded into her brown hair and draped over her bare shoulders are long white strings of dental floss.

"What the hell is going on here?" K tries to say, but her tongue flops huge and stupid in her mouth, slurring her words into nonsense.

Dr. Fred ignores K. His fingers swarm the keyboard, creating a symphony of clattering keystrokes. The woman in the hallway keeps rummaging through the supply closet.

Enraged by this nonsense and worried about her quickly swelling tongue, K climbs out of the dental chair and taps

Dr. Fred on the shoulder. When he doesn't turn around or acknowledge her presence, K looks at the computer. On the screen she sees a word document quickly filling with words. Thinking he's writing a report about the injury to her tongue, K reads a few lines.

and then the incredibly sexy and naughty dental assistant who just can't get enough of the studly doctor Frankfooter's superhot spankings goes over to the supply closet for more of the necessary unwaxed dental floss and

"My God," K grunts to herself, her tongue too swollen to fit inside her mouth anymore. "This is an office for children! How sick can you be?"

Disgusted that she's ever associated herself with these people, K turns around and walks toward the exit of the office. But before she can leave the exam room, the woman in the turquoise scrubs appears in the doorway and blocks her path.

"Please be patient, Mrs. K," The woman says, her voice pleasant and professional. The top of her scrubs is still missing. "Dr. Frankfooter is just about to start the procedure."

K gapes at the woman in disbelief and points to her own aching mouth. Like a dead animal draped over a hunter's shoulder, K's massive tongue hangs limp and heavy, its pink mass extending down to her waist.

"Can you not see this? I have to go to the hospital!" K says, her words tumbling from her mouth as garbled gibberish.

"Yes, I agree, it's a beautiful tongue," the woman says, smiling at K. "The studly Dr. Frankfooter does wonderful work. He's a great, great man."

The woman lets out a contented sigh and walks past K and leans her head on Dr. Fred's shoulder. Then she wraps her arms around his chest and stares at the screen as he continues his furious typing. Sensing her opportunity to escape this place, K hurries down the hallway and strides into the lobby. But just before she arrives at the front door of the office, the woman in the turquoise scrubs screams at her from behind.

"You goddamn little thief!" the woman shouts, her voice scratchy and shrill. "I know exactly what you're doing. Using your feminine wiles to con my studly Dr. Frankfooter into giving you tongue-augmentation surgery for free. Disgusting. I bet you think you're so smart. But I've got news for you, lady. You're not going to get away with it this time."

Strings of dental floss flutter from the woman's shoulders as she darts past K with surprising speed. Before K can react, the woman shoves a heavy couch in front of the exit and clambers over the vacant reception desk. In seconds the woman is screaming into the telephone, demanding that the police arrest the dangerous individual who is burglarizing her dental office.

In a panic K presses her shoulder against the couch and starts to push. But the drool dripping from her massive tongue slicks the wood floor with liquid, and she crashes to the ground. Soon the quiet calm of the office fills with the wail of approaching police sirens.

K scrambles to her hands and knees and heaves her gargantuan tongue over her shoulder. As she pushes the couch out of the way, she feels a series of sharp jabs in her arms and legs. Looking around the lobby for the source, K sees the woman in the turquoise scrubs sitting on the edge of the reception desk. The woman is talking on the phone and lazily winging pens at K.

"Yup, uh huh, sure thing, baby," the woman says in a bored monotone. She flings a blue gel pen at K's knee and runs her hand through her tangled brown hair. Strands of dental floss float to the desk like oblong snowflakes.

With the woman distracted, K bursts through the front door and scrambles out into the night. The woman in the turquoise scrubs watches without interest and picks up a black pen and tosses it at K's back. The pen plinks against the wall beside the door and falls between the cushions of the couch. The woman sighs into the phone.

"Yeah, we should be done soon, baby. The last patient we had was a nightmare. Just wait until you hear the kind of nonsense she tried to pull. It's absolutely incredible. I swear. Sometimes these people make me want to slam my head against the wall. It's so frustrating."

Posted by u/samuraijake14 - 2 hours ago
Does anyone else have this problem or is it just me?

ok so i know this is going to sound super weird and stuff but please just try to bear with me because ive never asked strangers on reddit for advice like this but i swear this is a serious question and im not trolling because this is a real thing that happens to me all the time now and i dont know how to fix it and im too scared to ask my friends or parents about it because of what they might say. Ok so what i wanted to ask is if anyone else gets too scared to poop because they are afraid that a snake will crawl up out of the toilet hole while their sitting there with nothing to protect their bits. im asking because a few days ago i saw a story online (it was on msn or yahoo or someother place that talks about real news, so i think its true) about this woman who was in the bathroom of her house in florida and then she lifted up the toilet lid to do her business but before she sat down she saw a big snake crawling up out of the hole in her toilet where the poop gets flushed away and it turns out that something had happened to the pipes under her house and the snake got in from there and then it crawled all the way up into her toilet from the back. so i guess my question is if anyone else ever sees something like that and gets so scared and cant stop thinking about it to the point that they now cant do even the most normal things in their life like pooping because ever since i read that story i get really scared when i feel the need to poop because what if something like that happens to me? BTW im 14M and i live in northern florida (talahassee area) so its not like i live right next door to the toilet snake lady, but i do live in the same state so i cant stop thinking that if something so scary like that can happen to a random lady who lives kind of close, then whats stopping something like that from happening to me? now anytime i even think about pooping my mind goes crazy on its own and instantly imagines the most horrible thing that could possibly happen like the other day when i was at my friend terrys house and i needed to go to the bathroom, but then right after i got there and closed the door i saw a mind movie of me sitting on the toilet and getting bitten on the butt by a snake coming up out of the toilet hole and it was really scary because my mind showed me all the horrible details even tho i didnt want it to and even after i tried really hard to think about something else i couldnt and instead i just kept seeing the horrible mind movie of me getting bitten and my body starting to shake and jerk from the poison and me smashing my face against the hard floor and my teeth hitting the tiles really hard and breaking all over the place and it seemed so real that i could almost feel it happening and then in the mind movie i started throwing up uncontrollably and blood was everywhere and in the movie i knew i was dying so i started yelling for my mom because i was so scared and then no matter how hard the real me tried to think of something else, like fortnite or the new slipknot song or that awsome fight with levi from attack on titan, i couldnt stop seeing myself dying horribly and it was so awful to the point that in real life i started crying and i could barely breathe and it was so embarassing because terry had to call my mom and ask her to come pick me up and even after mom was there i couldnt stop my body from shaking so i just spent the rest of the day in bed and i didnt go to school the next day. i only ask these things because that day was one of the worst in my entire life and im shaking right now just thinking about it but a similar thing happens now every time i have to poop and i dont know what to do or how to make it go away. i know this post has been rambling on for a while and im sorry about that but i just get so incredibly scared sometimes about all the awful stuff in the news and about all the terrible things that could happen to me and my friends and family and i cant stop wondering why everyone is always arguing so much about stuff that seems really obvious like how the other day when my english teacher mrs collins told the class that men and women are exactly the same in every single way, but how is that even possible when girls have lady bits and guys have dongs and girls can get pregnant and guys cant? literally everyone already knows that stuff so why would she even say something that everyone already knows is wrong? so i guess my real question is just why is everything in the world so confusing and scary? also any tips re: my pooping dilemma would be cool thx

You'll Never Leave

At twenty-seven my body began to vanish. First it was small things I barely missed, like the runty little nail on my left pinky toe, or the shaggy coat of hair on my right calf, but after a while more important things started disappearing. Soon it was the disk of cartilage in my left knee, the pad of fat sheathed within my right heel. And as if that wasn't enough, each time something vanished, I would suddenly wake up on the concrete floor of my basement with no memory of how I got there.

It was summer. I was still living with my parents then, not sure of what to do with my life. In college I'd studied anthropology, and during those years I'd dreamed of someday traveling the world and immersing myself in the different cultures of mankind, but by the time I graduated I was already thirty grand in debt, so that never panned out. Instead, I spent the next six years sliding gallons of milk into metal racks in the forty-degree dairy cooler of my hometown Value King supermarket.

Later, once my body started vanishing, I realized I'd had enough of that cooler, so I quit the next day.

My parents went to London for vacation that August. At the time I hadn't yet told them about my vanishing body, so they let me stay behind and house sit.

While they were gone I looked for a new job. I was so sick of living at home and feeling like a failure, so I scoured the internet for something full-time and sustainable, something that would finally let me escape the prison that was my parents' house.

A few days later I got called in for an interview at the Topine Free Library. The interview was for a full-time library assistant job, and it was the only paid position available that didn't require a Master's degree, so for once I was actually qualified for the job I was applying for. By then my entire right leg was gone except for the skin, but I didn't care about that for the moment. The only thing that mattered was my interview. So to help me get around my buddy Colin let me borrow a pair of crutches from the hospital where he worked.

Around eight-thirty on the morning of my interview, I crutched into the kitchen to grab some milk from the fridge. Moments later I woke up in the basement. When I tried to stand up, I discovered a bag of empty skin piled in the place where my left leg used to be.

Now the severity of my situation finally set in. I tore through my flattened pockets in a panic, searching for my phone. Then I remembered: I'd left it on the dresser in my bedroom upstairs.

From here I tried to calm myself with some deep breaths. When that didn't work, I lay back on the cold concrete and stared up at the ceiling. There I saw the bones of my missing toes bracing the sagging pipes above. I saw the fibrous ropes of my tendons holding the furnace's tube in place. I saw the pad of fat from my heel jammed into a leaky crack in the wood.

For the next hour I looked around for the rest of me. I wasn't able to find everything I'd lost, but by then it didn't matter because I finally understood. This place would never let me leave.

There's a Crashing Plane Behind the Store

Moments after Leni clocks in for her afternoon shift at the pharmacy, Daisy taps her on the shoulder.

"So did you see the plane yet?" Daisy says.

"What plane?"

"There's a crashing plane stuck in the woods behind the store," Amber says from her workstation at the end of the counter, her latex-gloved fingers dancing across her keyboard.

"My God," Leni says. "Is anyone hurt?"

"It's just an art project, it's not real," Glen says from behind. "Dennis was just in here a few minutes ago picking up his dad's medication, and he told me his troopers have found these things all over town. At least ten of them. Just before lunch they found a frozen 737 plowed into the ground behind Value King across the street. He said it's probably just a weird artist trying to do some kind of viral-marketing, Banksy-type thing."

"I don't understand what any of you are talking about. Is anyone hurt or not?" Leni says, as she tries, and fails, to log into her workstation. All this talk about crashing planes sends her heart galloping, her fingers trembling, her anxiety churning. When no one answers her question, she closes her eyes, reaches into her pocket, and wraps her fingers around the bottle of Klonopin she keeps with her at all times in case of a panic attack. Feeling the familiar shape of that smooth cylinder resting in the fleshy pocket of skin between her thumb and index finger, her heart starts to slow a bit.

"Banksy is that British artist who makes crazy stuff like this," Glen says. "He paints fake doors into concrete walls and draws pictures of little girls in gas masks. It's political commentary. But if that's what this guy is doing, I don't get it. I don't understand what a plane crash behind a CVS is supposed to mean."

Now Daisy rests a hand on Leni's shoulder.

"Let's go take a look," Daisy says. "Nobody's hurt, I promise. You'll feel better if you see it for yourself."

A computerized voice speaks from the phone next to Glen.

One pharmacy call.

"I'm coming too," Amber says, snapping off her latex

gloves. "I didn't get to take any pictures last time."

"Two minutes," Glen says, picking up his phone and clamping the handset between his ear and shoulder. "If you're not back in two minutes, I'm going to come out there and drag you back in here myself. Just because we don't have any customers at the moment doesn't mean you can all stand around and gawk at that plane. We've got scripts to fill and pills to count."

#

A minute later Leni steps into the rear parking lot and looks to the woods behind the store. There she sees a jumbo jet frozen in mid-air, its gleaming white nosecone aimed straight at the back wall of the store. The plane is huge, almost as big as the entire building, and it hovers less than thirty feet above the ground. The plane's left wing has been ripped in half by a giant sugar maple standing at the edge of the woods. The massive engine that was connected to that wing now lays crumpled on the pavement at the far end of the parking lot. Frozen orange flames like glass knives jut from the front and sides of the ruined engine.

Looking at the plane and its frozen wreckage, Leni's heart starts its heavy thudding once again. Is she really the only one who is scared of this thing?

"Huh," Daisy says, craning her head to the side. "Wasn't it farther back in the woods last time we were out here?"

"I didn't get a chance to take any pictures last time, so I have no idea. Here," Amber says, handing her phone to Leni. "I want to try that forced perspective thing people do on Instagram where it looks like they're holding the Washington Monument in the palm of their hand."

From here Amber and Daisy jog out into the parking lot and hold up their hands under the plane. Once they get the positioning right, they turn to Leni. With her pulse thumping in her ears, Leni zooms out until it looks like the two women are holding the frozen plane in the palms of their hands.

"Okay, that looks good," Leni says. "Smile."

An instant before Leni presses the shutter button, a shard of orange flame sprouts from the ruined engine on the ground.

"Did you just—" Leni says, her breath catching in her

throat. The two women jog back to where Leni is standing.

"Did you get it?" Amber says.

Leni hands over the phone and looks at the engine again. It is completely still. Nothing in that area is moving except for the wind-jostled branches of the oaks, the teardrop leaves of the elms. Due to the reality distorting powers of her anxiety, Leni knows she can't always trust her own senses, but still she can't look away. Something in her head keeps telling her that plane is dangerous.

"Oh nice," Amber says, staring down at her phone. Now she shows the picture to Daisy. "Are you sure that thing is safe?" Leni says, her eyes fixed on the frozen plane.

Daisy looks back at the plane.

"Len, it's fine. It's just a sculpture."

"But I think it just moved."

"It probably did," Amber says, slipping her phone into the front pocket of her navy-blue scrubs. "Doesn't Banksy do all kinds of crazy stuff like that with his art just to screw with people? That's probably what this guy did, since he's a copycat."

The store's back door swings open.

"Time's up!" Glen says, shouting across the parking lot. "Let's get a move on, ladies, we've got customers!"

"Well, that was fun," Amber says, as her and Daisy start trotting to the door.

"You have to send that picture to me," Daisy says to Amber. "My girls will get a kick out of it."

"Tell Glen I'll be there in a second," Leni says, but neither Daisy nor Amber seem to hear her.

Now Leni jogs up to the ruined jet engine and runs her fingertips along an intact section of the mangled sheet metal. It feels smooth, cool, authentic. From what she can tell it seems to be made out of real metal, not some other material an artist would use to build an imitation. Feeling this, her heart begins to beat faster. To calm herself down she rests her hand on one of the glinting shards of frozen flame. The flame is cold, as smooth as volcanic glass; it gleams as brilliantly as a cut gem; the edges are as sharp as sawblades. But it is still. Everything is still.

With her hand resting on the flame, Leni closes her eyes. Here she tells herself that this is just art, that she is no longer an ER nurse, that no one is going to die because of this. Soon her heart begins to slow. A blue jay chirps overhead. The heat of the afternoon sun warms her cheek. A cool breeze grazes her ears, her nose, the backs of her fingers.

Seconds later she cries out in pain and jerks her hand from the frozen flame. Now she looks down at her palm and sees a shiny pink burn mark forming on her skin. Seeing this, she doesn't waste another moment. She runs across the parking lot to the back door, the soles of her padded running shoes snapping against the pavement. As she streaks into the store, she prays to God that she can find the words to reach them, to make them finally understand the danger they are in.

To You, in Another 31 Years

For thirty-one days you've been trapped inside this house, searching for an exit. There is a part of you that craves this idea of freedom more than anything, but you can feel that part slowly suffocating on the stale, dusty air of this quiet place. The other parts of you, the animal parts that speak in the wordless languages of fear and self-preservation, they are taking over.

And it's because of them that you do the strange things you do these days. It's because of them that you spend your mornings standing in a dark corner of a room in a dark corner of the house. There you watch bricks of buttery light slanting across the floor, schools of tiny motes shuddering in the yellow glow. These things are comforting to you. They let you know, in a safe way, that there is still an entire world outside these walls, and that you are still a discrete thing that has not yet disappeared from that world, not completely.

Despite this comfort, you are afraid of the light. You are afraid of the obliterating brightness, the destructive heat, the power it has to scatter your body to a puddle of flickering particles. You only need to look to the empty space at the end of your left wrist to remember what the light can do to you.

And then there are the things that hide in the light, the things you see if you look directly into it: spidery figures climbing spike-topped mountains, intrepid adventurers exploring lush green forests, skilled musicians stuffing dark rooms with sound. Living outside the house, drenched in the light, these people seem to exist on a different plane of being from you. Even if you could find an exit, you don't see how you'd ever be able to move fast enough to survive in that world.

So you stay in the dark. It's safer there anyway. You walk the shadowed hallways slowly and feel the cool floorboards bending beneath your feet. Sometimes, when you get too tired to keep searching for an exit, or when the light cuts off your passage, you sprawl on the floor and stare up at the white slab of the ceiling. From here you listen to the creaking of the old wood, the crackling of the dimpled plaster, the hissing silence in your ears, and in this way the minutes pass. You feel them sweeping over your body, flying low, gently grazing your lips, and for a few short seconds you are happy. The frightened animal parts of you finally calm down. The speed and heat and white-flash brightness of the light is far away. Now you close your eyes and listen as the animal parts tell you that this is right, that this is what you should be doing, that this is what you would be dreaming of doing if you ever did find a way out of the house. The minute you step out there, they say, you'd be wishing you were back here, where things are cool and calm and quiet. It's not a crime that this is how you like things to be. There's nothing wrong with wanting different things than everyone else.

As you listen to them saying this, it starts to feel true, if only partly. There is still that small slice of you that knows this place is a prison, but that part is very weak and the voice it speaks in is very quiet and the only time you can hear it whispering to you is in the silences between breaths. And so, instead of searching for an exit in the light-drenched living room at the end of the hallway, you take the advice of the louder, more persistent voice, and spend the rest of your thirty-first day in the house laying on the floor in the hallway.

When you wake up the next morning, you see that the house has changed around you. The hallway is narrower. The ceiling is lower and veined with long, branching, hair-thin cracks. The light-drenched living room at the end of the hallway is now a tiny half-bathroom with a marble sink. Clambering to hand and knees, you feel the cold floorboards pressing against your one remaining palm. Soon a rumbling vibration climbs up your arm. Now you look around and see that the ceiling is sliding downward and will soon crush you to death. From here the animal voices in your head scream at you to get back to the room at the corner of the house. They tell you to haul your ass under the bed inside that room if you want to survive this, but as you scrabble down the hallway, knees and elbows banging against the hard floorboards, you discover a small square window that was not there yesterday. A sharp-edged block of light shines through the window and in this light you see a wide, rolling field of soft green grass and lemon-yellow wildflowers. You stop in the hallway and look from this window to the doorway of the room and then down to the stump of your left wrist. You know what the light can do to you. You're looking at the carnage with your own eyes. But for some reason, you now have a strong feeling that this injury is an illusion of some kind, a distortion caused by the animal parts of you that are too afraid to leave the house.

Now you have a decision to make. I can't make it for you. I only hope that you can do what I could not, and you can find a way to overcome the parts of yourself that keep us forever trapped inside this house.

At Action Park

At the end of the summer, me and Kyoko went to Action Park for some fun. While waiting in line for the Tarzan swing, we met a girl named Gretchen who was in love with the alpine slide. She called the slide George and said it was her husband. Then she turned her leg to the side and showed us a road burn on her inner thigh that she said she got from the last time her and George had fucked. As the line inched out of the shade and into the sun, me and Kyoko asked Gretchen about her marriage with George: when they had met, how they fell in love, what their first time was like. Me and Kyoko had smoked a little weed on the drive over, and this was just the kind of silliness we were looking for on our last day-trip together.

In two days, me and Kyoko would be heading off for college on opposite sides of the country. I was going to study music in upstate New York, and Kyoko had earned a scholarship to study criminal justice in California. Though Kyoko had assured me that nothing would change between us because of the distance, I was worried. After more than three years together, I'd learned that I needed her much more than she needed me.

Once the three of us had taken our rides on the Tarzan swing, we decided to spend the rest of the day together. Gretchen was all alone, and she was fun to talk to, so we said why not.

At noon we sat in board shorts and bikinis in the open-air restaurant at the center of the park. There we ate thick slices of pizza topped with fat knobs of sausage, towering ice cream sundaes drowned in hot fudge and sprinkles.

At sunset we smoked a j in the back of Gretchen's station wagon and listened to one of my Bill Evans cassettes. Bill Evans was my favorite jazz pianist ever, and I practiced piano for over two hours a day in the hopes that someday I'd be able to write something as brilliant as "Waltz for Debby."

As me and Kyoko watched the sky burn with streaks of red and pink and orange and purple, Gretchen reached under the seat and pulled out a gun and started to cry. Through her tears she told us that George had broken up with her last night, and that she had been waiting all day for the park to close so she could climb into George's mouth and shoot herself in the head. My brain was too slowed by the weed to react to any of this, but

Kyoko grabbed the gun from Gretchen's hand and pushed open the back door with her bare foot. Kyoko's dad had been a homicide detective for over twenty years, so she knew the right way to handle a gun.

Kyoko walked Gretchen toward the woods behind the empty parking lot. Cool evening air sliced past my face as I climbed out of the car and clambered after them. Standing at the edge of the woods, Kyoko emptied the three bullets into Gretchen's palm and whispered something into her ear. Gretchen nodded and threw the bullets into the woods and wrapped her arms around Kyoko's shoulders and cried. The sun slipped behind the trees. Mosquitos needled my bare shoulders. Kyoko looked at me with a half-smile, as if she was thinking about something good. Soon me and Kyoko would have to go back to the car and say our goodbyes to Gretchen, and to Action Park, and not long after, to each other, but right now, we didn't have to do anything.

Work-Life Balance

Work-life balance is key it's essential for anyone who wants to last in this line of work ladies said Prof Gardner last night ending class early and now with crispy curled leaves crunching under her hiking boots Amanda thinks these words again while her eyes behind square glasses scan the forest trail for unearthed roots to hook a toe on

last thing she needs another injury left knee never right after that game against Oneonta senior year dirty fucking tackle that bitch not even aiming for the ball and for what they didn't even win nine-year ache hurts every day even on soft ground like this

trail a muddy ribbon unfurling between the trees under the quilted mat of leaves already dead before they hit the ground their brittle bodies dried stiff bled crimson spotted with crumbly brown spots the decay the worst there this is what she sees when she looks at the world these days death and disintegration everywhere even her boots the ones Joe had bought for her twenty- ninth last year *for all that hiking you want to do* cheap boots from a cheap guy fake leather starting to crack while he's off with his new wife or girlfriend or whatever the fuck

that woman is to him by now Amanda can't remember the one in the picture his latest profile picture the two of them grinning in front of a house a colonial of some kind her hair stubbornly perfect despite the rainy day under iron skies French or Dutch or German was the house one of those but who knows she can't remember which

just another thing she used to care about that's nothing to her now those real estate days career number two or maybe it was three *she's beautiful* Amanda had said leaning over her keyboard staring at the woman's face inside the glowing screen inside the cropped picture some lost night when she should have been trying to sleep a dream she can remember would be nice

an easy night's sleep some time away from her life yes nice some time would be nice been a while since she cared enough to check Joe's Facebook probably the summer at least back before she started up with her new classes for her new career number five this one is her new career in nursing for her new life of selflessness helping others instead of herself but of course it's all bullshit just code for more searching desperate to feel alive desperate to feel happy to feel love for something again standing before the full length mirror in her bedroom with her nurse scrubs on the lie a living thing *if I can't even be honest with myself than what can I* said out loud to herself but didn't know how to end the sentence Joe's Facebook definitely a while since she checked but who cares that stuff is for people who have the *life* part of the work- life balance

essential for anyone who wants to last probably meant for everyone those words but Amanda knew who Prof Gardener was talking to when she said it staring hard at Amanda Prof Gardner's eyes speaking in silence *this is the important stuff so pay attention all that anatomy chemistry skeletal structure can wait but this is what you really need to know* her eyes saying it just like that staring right at Amanda in the back of the classroom the old woman's voice rusty and dull her eyes even worse just black beads at a distance the eyes telling Amanda the truth she already knew *you're not going to last* a froggy voice lined with gravel or hard crumbs of stale bread like Amanda always used to say to her mom when she was sick with a sore throat *it feels like hard crumbs got stuck*

or when she was too afraid to go to school too afraid to see those nasty bitches who were supposed to be her friends she would say it then too because why do they do that not just girls but all people so much goddamn talking but no one telling the truth everything so distorted so many lies can't tell anymore what's real and what's not who's lying and who's not what's the right thing to do with so many people suffering and she does want to help but

yes this is what she came out here to do sort all this out for good so many years of unhappiness a life of it just everything so empty all the juice squeezed out of everything she ever loved but yes that's right at one time there were things she loved she can remember it now as she takes the right path of the trail forking around a knotty oak or maybe a maple red maple sugar maple who cares she can't tell without any leaves on the bare branches and looking up hot yellow light flashes between wooden fingers

but yes a time when she did love something that did happen she's sure of it yes a good place to start because from there maybe she can trace a line to where she is now that's one thing that's true there was a time when she did love some things a few people all those stupid pages in her middle school diary *I love Karl S.!!!!!* the asterisk-like stars she used to draw around the words her younger self believing that those things made her love even more special but to love something is special yes it was special that

cold sparkling numbing syrup that used to drip down over her stomach each time she talked to those boys she loved Karl S.!!!!!Tom C.!!!!!Will N.!!!!!Jesse D.!!!!! all of them she did she loved them so easy it was so simple it happened just like that like getting hit out of nowhere lightning is what they always say it's like one day she was just herself and then it hit her and she finally saw him Karl S. Jesse D. whoever else so many too many to remember and now none all that electricity gone but back then out of nowhere it would happen so sudden his incredible

specialness suddenly visible in a way no one else could see only her she could see it and oh how deep it went all the way down to the marrow in her toes she could feel it all those feelings inside her yes it was real and this memory is

just a tiny sliver of what it felt like remembering it in her head thinking it back into the present and now coming to a place on the trail where a hard rectangle of sun cuts through the naked canopy and stamps a sharp square of light on the trail and

seeing this she stops and looks at the little bits of dust or dirt floating in the shaft of light her eyes starting to burn tears coming from somewhere a small bright feeling inside and suddenly she is so joyfully happy to be alive but the second she thinks this her awareness of the feeling makes it fake and blinking from the collecting tears it's gone already just that quick one blink two it's gone buried so far that it's like it was never even here and

walking on she steps through the light into the gray shadow of the lack left over and the absence in her chest is so wide and deep and empty that she doesn't even want to do this anymore *why even try* why even be here in the woods by herself why does this always happen it never works nothing ever works why does she feel this way why can't she feel anymore no love for anything why can't she just be happy like everyone else her classmates all these girls so happy always smiling laughing all the time making jokes but she can't everything is fake her words her smiles she feels it on her face her lips carved and shining like the old wax candy the acting always acting always sitting alone in the last row back of the classroom *always have an escape route* why couldn't she just ask them last night *do you want to go for a hike tomorrow* but yes that's right she didn't ask because she didn't want them to come more acting more trying she didn't and did and didn't but still does and doesn't and does doesn't make sense never did can't explain it to Linda if she doesn't understand it herself too much thinking too much acting she gets so tired pretending that everything is okay not hollow there has to be a reason why does this always happen to her everything squeezed dry when did the juice leak out can't remember when or how it happened but it's gone and dried up her insides hollow she feels the lack like

all those days she passed in bed more yellow light through the window another shining square on the floor her bed so cold body heavy legs tingling with ache it was her sister who had come that time Linda's shadow darkening the small space under the door talking through wood the closed door Linda knowing to not even ask if she could open it

maybe you should talk to someone
I have
a therapist I mean someone like that
I have one I used to but it didn't help
maybe try a different one it can take some time to find the right one
I have Amanda said knowing it was a lie but also the truth already the next question she knew what her sister would ask before the words came out anger scudding up her throat because no one fucking understands empty when something is empty and nothing can fill it back up yet they keep trying these people always trying

why not
a therapist can't live your life for you and now turning around and walking through the shaft of light again the trail the woods Amanda starts the walk back to her car parked in the lot of that warehouse lumber or shipping the warehouse across the street from the entrance to the woods

just another car what do they care at least some people know how to not care to not try at least in that she's not alone so much trying too much five careers never knew when to stop and now trudging back to the car a chilly breeze in her face brittle leaves rustling like paper the smell of the trees in her nose sharp and peppery like cracked cinnamon sticks this light the quiet the peace yes it's pretty very beautiful but what can she do with it can't take it home can't absorb it inside can't do anything with it have to leave it here the lack

just a normal thing now and still the same an hour later when she climbs into her car in the warehouse lot key slides into ignition engine growls a cool sigh from deep in her lungs *yes I did try I did* for five careers she did and back in here she almost feels normal again normal but a little lighter than before another thing gone but who cares less weight to carry less gravity less pull *God knows I tried* the last words she speaks before pulling out of the lot and turning left instead of right right leading home left to somewhere else doesn't matter where somewhere away from here *essential for anyone who wants to last ladies* Prof Gardner had said *for anyone who wants to last* yes the old woman had been right saw it from the start knew Amanda wouldn't last but yes she had tried at least she had tried

Monday Morning at the Office

George arrived at the office a few minutes early this morning, so he headed over to the employee break room to grab some breakfast before starting his day. The hardwood floorboards swished cold and smooth beneath the soles of his bare feet, and from the way the wintery chill seeped into his skin and settled into the marrow of his aching knees, he could tell the new office manager had forgotten to turn the heat on.

When George stepped into the employee break room, he saw a man sitting at the lunch table, eating a bowl of corn flakes. George had never seen this man before, but from the rumors he'd recently heard floating around the hallways, he figured this had to be Greene's new office manager. For the past few days, everyone around the office, including George, had been in an uproar over how young and inexperienced Greene's new office manager was rumored to be, and now, finally meeting the man face to face, George felt even more angry. This man looked to be no older than thirty or thirty-five, nearly twenty years younger than George's fifty-four. And as if that wasn't infuriating enough, this kid had come into work wearing nothing but a pair of old sweatpants and a ratty white t-shirt with a stretched-out collar. Seeing this, George clenched his teeth and made a mental note to have a serious talk with his son Randall this afternoon after the boy's track meet. Young men need discipline and structure, and this dunce sitting before him was living proof that twelve years old was absolutely not too early to start educating his boy about professionalism and accountability in the workplace.

"Morning Dad," the new office manager said to George. "How are you feeling today?"

A thick fog of anger collected in George's head as he walked over to the toaster oven in the corner of the room. A jar of grape jam, a freshly sliced bagel, and a clean butter knife sat neatly arranged on the counter in front of the toaster. While George's hands picked up the bagel, slipped it into the toaster, and set the dial to medium-brown, he turned his head and fixed an angry stare at the kid sitting at the table.

"That's how you show up for work on your first day?" George said to the new office manager. "In your goddamn underwear?"

"Oh okay, so we're at the office already," the new office manager said, nodding to himself. "Got it."

"It's six fifty-one on Monday morning. Where the hell else would we be?" George said.

As George turned back to the toaster, he caught a glimpse of his stalker watching him through the break room window. The image had been nothing more than a flicker of movement in the dark, a split-second flash of a pair of eyes behind the glass, but George knew his stalker was out there. He had seen those gray-blue eyes so many times over the past year he'd be able to recognize them in his sleep. So to throw that murderous bastard off his trail, George pretended he hadn't seen anything, and instead waited for the heating bars inside the toaster to glow a brilliant, neon orange.

"You're right, George, I'm sorry about that," the new office manager said. "My dad always told me that the best way to get ahead in life is to keep my mouth shut and my ears open, so I'll be sure to do that from now on."

"Damn right. I tell my boy the exact same thing every day. Not sure how good he listens since he's only twelve, but I still make sure to tell him," George said. "Your father sounds like a smart man."

"Yeah," the new office manager said, looking at George with a tired smile. "He was."

George noticed that the new office manager's eyes had suddenly gone red and watery, as if the man was about to cry, so he looked away. Public displays of emotion had always made him uncomfortable. But when he saw the man's dreadful personal appearance for a second time, his anger rushed back in an instant.

"Too bad he didn't teach you anything about professionalism or presenting yourself in the right way."

"Yeah," the new office manager said, turning back to his cereal. His voice was quiet and thin. "I overslept this morning, so I didn't have the chance to get every single thing ready for you. Sorry about that."

George shook his head in disgust.

"Well, excuses are like assholes. Everybody's got one. And if you think me or Howard Greene or anyone else in this office is going to tolerate excuses, you've got another thing coming."

George looked down at the toaster. Though the dial was still set on medium brown, the heating bars inside the toaster were black and cold. Seeing this, he figured it was done toasting. So he removed his cold bagel, picked up the grape jam and the knife, and walked over to the lunch table.

As George passed the window, he saw his stalker once again. And as usual, the bastard was mocking him, imitating his exact actions as he walked past the window. But this time the psycho took things a step further. Somehow that asshole had acquired a set of exact replicas of everything George was holding in his hands at this moment: the plate, the knife, the grape jam, everything. Even the goddamn bagel!

Despite his surprise, George was ready for this gambit. That bastard had been trying to kill him for over a year, so by now nothing he did would ever catch George off guard. And thanks to his past experience with this psycho, George knew exactly how to get rid of him: the police. One call to the police and the stalker would have to engage his alien cloaking device to avoid capture, which would then drain the device's battery and force him to return to his hideout for ten minutes so it could recharge.

With all this in mind, George sat down at the table across from the new office manager. Then he leaned forward and spoke as quietly as he could to the man.

"I know this is your first day on the job, but you need to shut your mouth and listen to me very carefully," George said. He darted his eyes to the slab of black-blue sky visible through the break room window. "There's a man outside that window who is trying to kill me. He is very dangerous and has access to alien technology that is more advanced than anything the human race can possibly imagine. The only way to make him go away is to call the police as soon as possible. If we do that, he'll have to engage his alien cloaking device to avoid capture, which will quickly drain the battery and force him to return to his hideout while the device recharges."

The new office manager let out an anguished sigh and looked up at the ceiling. Moments later George noticed two shining trails of tears crawling down the man's face, but George didn't feel any sympathy for him. This is exactly what happens when you steal your job from a more qualified man instead of working for it like everybody else.

"Oh my God," the new office manager said. "I can't do this anymore, Dad. I'm sorry, but I just can't do it."

"Then why the hell did you take this job in the first place you disrespectful little shit!" George said, picking up his plate and winging it at the new office manager's head. The plate whizzed past the kid's ear like a frisbee and shattered against the wall behind. "I've been working with Howard Greene for over seventeen years! I was supposed to be the next manager of this office! Me! *Two years ago* he promised me that position! That was my promotion before you came in here and sucked him off in the supply closet to weasel your way in! And as if that wasn't enough, I've got this psycho bastard out here trying to kill me for over a year, and still I come into work every goddamn day! Risking my life to put food on the table for my wife and son!"

Without a word the new office manager walked around the table, pulled George out of his chair, and shoved him toward the window.

"Get your hands off me!" George said. He kicked and punched the new office manager as hard as he could, but nothing worked. The kid held him in a bear hug as tight as a steel vice. As they approached the window, George felt a wave of cold terror crash over him.

"You fucking bastard," George said, his body quivering in fear. "You're in on it aren't you? You goddamn rat. I should've known that bastard wasn't working alone. No wonder you got that job instead of me. So, what's the plan? Are you going to kill Howard Greene too? Are you two just going to kill everyone in this office to make sure you don't get caught?"

"No one is trying to kill you," the new office manager said into George's ear. He positioned George in front of the break room window and gripped the back of his head and forced him to look outside. But when George looked through the glass, all he saw was that murderous bastard with the gray-blue eyes staring back at him. "Nobody is out there. That's the reflection of your own face in the glass."

Hearing this, the murderous bastard widened his eyes in phony terror and turned his face away, mocking George with a clownish impression of his own fear.

"Bullshit!" George said, whipping his head backward as hard as he could. A dry crack rang out from somewhere behind. A sharp needle of pain bored into the back of his head. The new office manager let out a wet groan, released George from the bear hug, and crumpled to the floor. Then, as the kid groaned on the floor, thick red blood pouring from his broken nose, George slipped through the door of the break room and shuffled down the hallway toward his cubicle. But since those two murderous bastards had turned out all the lights in the office, George quickly lost his way in a dizzying maze of dark corridors and unfamiliar rooms.

George frantically searched for a way to escape, but nothing made sense. Every hallway he stumbled down looked the same. Each door he came across stood as an unmarked mystery. And no matter how many rooms he checked, he couldn't find the exit. Instead, every door he opened somehow led back to the same two rooms: a reeking bedroom with an old man's clothes strewn about the floor, a white-tile bathroom with a small door built into the side of the bathtub.

After another minute of terrified confusion, George admitted to himself that those murderous bastards had trapped him. So he closed himself off in the white-tile bathroom and started yelling for help. He knew it was a longshot, but he hoped Rodger or Pete would show up late as usual and hear him calling. Maybe then they would make themselves useful for once and rescue him before the murdering psychos could kill them too.

For the next few minutes, George sat on the cold tile of the bathroom and yelled for help. No one came. He was completely alone.

But that was okay because soon he realized it was time to head off to work, so he stood up, stepped out of the bathroom, and started his morning commute to the office.

#

George arrived at the office a few minutes early this morning, so he headed over to the employee break room to grab some breakfast before starting his day. The hardwood floorboards swished cold and smooth beneath the soles of his bare feet, and from the way the wintery chill seeped into his skin and settled into the marrow of his aching knees, he could tell the new office manager had forgotten to turn the heat on.

When George stepped into the employee break room, he saw a man sitting at the lunch table, holding a wad of bloody napkins to his face. George had never seen this man before, but from the rumors he'd recently heard floating around the hallways, he figured this had to be Greene's new office manager.

Before George could say a word, the man stood up and removed the napkins from his face. An upside down, black-red V of dried blood clung to the bridge of the man's severely crooked nose. Thick rings of purple flesh hung beneath his watery, bloodshot eyes. Despite this, he stared at George with a determination so fierce it bordered on rage. Seeing this, George knew in an instant that this man was Greene's new office manager. Though George couldn't imagine what had happened during the man's commute for him to show up to work in this state, he couldn't help but respect the man already. A real man doesn't make excuses, and George could tell from his stare alone that he'd never hear an excuse from this man. With all this in mind, George felt a little less angry about Greene breaking his word and giving the office manager promotion to this man instead of him.

"Good morning, George, I'm Randall," the man said, his voice thick and muffled from his injuries. He offered his hand for a handshake.

"Nice to meet you, Randall," George said, taking the man's hand and gripping it tightly. The man returned the pressure and then some. "That's a nice firm handshake you got there. And I like that name too. My son's name is Randall."

"I know."

"Is that so?" George said, with a smile and a nod. He was liking this kid more and more by the second. Natural born leader. No wonder Greene hired him. "Did some research on your men before coming into the office? I like the sound of that."

"A real man takes his job seriously. That's what my dad always taught me."

"Damn right. He sounds like a smart man."

"He was. But if it's alright with you I'd like to get started," Randall said, gesturing toward the doorway of the break room. "Mr. Greene just told me about an appraisal we've got scheduled for this morning at a business over in Topine, and I'd like to ride along with you and observe you in action."

"Who's the client?" George said. "What kind of business?"

Randall cleared his throat and looked down at the floor.

George followed his gaze and saw that the kid's hands were shaking.

"It's one of those elderly care places," Randall said. "A twenty-four-hour care facility for elderly people with brain issues like dementia."

George clicked his tongue and nodded.

"Oh okay, yup. Not surprising. Those places have accidents all the time. Lots of property damage," George said, fishing around in his pockets for his car keys. "Just let me find my keys and we'll be off."

"Actually, Mr. Greene said he'd prefer that I drive," Randall said, holding up a set of car keys. "That way you can go over the paperwork on the drive over."

George studied the kid's beat up face and wondered whether it was safe for him to be driving with injuries like that. But once again, the kid's determined expression quickly quelled his fears.

With that sorted out, George smiled and made his way to the door. "Sounds good. You're the boss, boss."

As he passed, he gave the kid a friendly thump on the shoulder. "What'd you say your name was again?"

"It's Randall."

"No kidding. My son's name is Randall," George said. "He's going to be thirteen in August."

The kid cleared his throat again and looked away.

"I know."

Auditing

My brother Stan sits in front of my bedroom window with a blanket draped over his head. A pair of binoculars poke out from underneath the blanket, and through these he stares out the window. It's just after seven on Monday morning.

"The black SUV is back," Stan whispers. A triangular wedge of gold light stretches across the blobby mass of his concealed body. "Oh Christ. This is the third day in a row it's been there. It's got to be Barry. I knew he'd find me. He told me I'd never get away."

Stan's an aspiring magician. Last year he signed a billion-year contract with the Church of Scientology to increase his confidence and to build connections in the industry, but he only lasted six months. Two weeks ago he showed up at my apartment at three a.m. with nothing but a small bug-out bag slung over his shoulder. He looked pale and gaunt, and his sharp cheekbones erupted like mountains from the wasteland of his malnourished face. Since then, he hasn't left my apartment once. Now he spends all his time staring out the window, terrified that his old auditor, Barry, will show up and threaten to reveal his darkest secrets to the world if he doesn't go back to Gold Base to clean toilets with a toothbrush.

I groan with exhaustion and stare at the white ceiling.

"Tell me again what I'm supposed to say if they call in on the intercom," I say.

"It doesn't matter what you say," Stan says. "They've already labeled you as an SP. In their eyes, you're a mortal enemy of the church. They won't believe a single word that comes out of your mouth. You just have to ignore them. They're going to lie and tell you crazy stories about me to try to harass you into telling them where I am, but please, Grant, don't listen to anything they say. Especially if they try to tell you things that they say I said about you. None of it's true, I swear. They just lie about everything."

Now that I'm fully awake, I sit up and stretch my sore neck.

"Sounds like someone I know."

Stan sighs.

"I admit that I may have stretched the truth on occasion

in the past, but I'm small-time compared to these people. They'll say anything to get what they want. They don't care how many lives they destroy. I, on the other hand, have a sense of loyalty to those I care about."

"But aren't you the one who got me labeled as a suppressive person to begin with? Who else could've told them I tried to stop you from signing the billion-year contract? Not even Mom wants anything to do with you anymore. She calls me every week to complain about you."

Stan's binoculars thump to the floor.

"Oh my God," Stan says, his voice quivering in panic. "It's Barry. He's here. He's walking up to the front of the building."

Stan grabs the ends of his blanket and runs into the kitchen.

A loud electronic buzz tears through the apartment.

I climb out of bed and walk to the front door. My neck hurts, my shoulders ache, and my legs burn from yesterday's long shift at the restaurant. Today was supposed to be my one chance this week to sleep in and recover from eight straight days of work on the line, but there's no way that's going to happen now. Wherever my brother goes, trouble always seems to follow. It's been that way ever since we were kids.

As I trudge past the kitchen, I see Stan frantically trying to pull open the locked window above the sink. But since my apartment is on the ground floor, the landlord permanently locked all the windows to prevent break-ins.

I step up to the front door. Just before I press the talk button on the intercom, I poke my head into the kitchen and press my finger to my lips for quiet.

Stan shakes his head and mouths some words at me.

Please don't.

For the first time since he showed up here, I start to wonder what Stan told Barry during their auditing sessions. He must've talked about me. But what did he say? What kind of secrets could an amateur magician possibly have, to make him so afraid of these people?

I press the talk button.

Stan runs back into the bedroom, the tail of his blanket fluttering like a cape.

"Who is this?" I say into the intercom, my pre-coffee

crankiness seeping into my voice. "Do you realize what time it is?"

"Good morning, Grant," a man's voice says. The voice is calm and patient and free of all emotion, like an airline pilot. "We're here for Stan. We know he's in there. Can you buzz us in, please?"

Before I can respond, I hear three loud thuds and a crash of crackling glass.

I run back to the kitchen. The early morning chill leaks through the broken window. The woody smell of autumn fills the room. On the floor, Stan's ruined binoculars lay among glittering shards of broken glass.

Another loud buzz tumbles through the apartment. But instead of returning to the front door, I retreat to the bedroom and call the police.

"I need to report a break-in," I say. "A man driving a black SUV broke the window in my kitchen, and now he's at my front door, trying to get inside my apartment."

The woman on the phone asks me my name, my location, whether I'm in immediate danger or not. While I answer these questions, I look out the window and try to predict where Stan will sleep tonight. Outside, a lone oak sways slowly in the breeze. The woman on the phone tells me to stay on the line.

Cryonics

Larry and his roommate Bart were driving to work in Larry's Toyota when they got to talking about death and reincarnation and things of that nature.

"If you died right now and had the chance to be reincarnated as anything in the entire world, what would it be?" Larry said, gripping the steering wheel loosely.

"Hmmm," Bart said. He scratched his wiry beard and looked out the passenger-side window. Crags of crusty snow sawed past on the side of the road while bony branches of leafless oaks shivered in the gray December morning. "If I had to come back as something, I'd probably want to be a 14/2 NM-B cable."

Both Larry and Bart were engineers: civil for Larry, electrical for Bart. Their respective offices stood less than five minutes away from each other, so they carpooled to work each morning to save gas.

"That's the dumbest thing I've ever heard in my life," Larry said with a scoff. "Of all the things you could come back as, why would you pick a copper wiring power cable or whatever that is?"

Bart grinned at Larry.

"Because then I'd be a light in the darkness for everyone in the entire world," Bart said. His grin grew wider for a moment, and then he looked up at the ceiling of the car and shook his head. "Actually, that's not true. I'm pretty sure they use different wire gauges in Europe and Asia. So in that case, I'd only be a light in the darkness for everyone in North America. But still. If I had to make a snap decision on the spot, I'd probably want to come back as that."

"That's such a stupid answer," Larry said, "but at least you have some logic behind it."

Bart laughed and fluttered his fingers in front of the dashboard heating vents.

Bart had been friends with Larry ever since they'd been lab partners in their freshman- year physics class at Topine Community College more than seven years ago. That semester, Bart and Larry had bonded over a shared love for psychedelics, retro video games, and philosophical thought experiments: Bart's three favorite ways to escape the brain-rotting mundanity of everyday life.

"Well, it's kind of hard to ponder the ultimate fate of my existence at eight thirty-six in the morning," Bart said, looking down at the glowing green digits of the dashboard clock. "But what about you?"

Larry lifted his right hand from the steering wheel and showed Bart a metal bracelet looped around his wrist.

"I'll be coming back as myself," Larry said. "I'm going to have my brain cryogenically frozen immediately after death so my consciousness can be uploaded into a computer in the distant future."

Bart craned his head to the side and looked at Larry's bracelet. Etched into the metal tag was a phone number, the name of a laboratory in New York City, and a short set of directions for medical personnel to follow in the event of Larry's death.

"Huh. A guy in my outfit wants to do the same thing, but everyone thinks he's a nutjob," Bart said, glancing out the window. He watched a red Honda sedan slip past in the right lane. "They all say it's bullshit. And expensive as hell."

"It's not bullshit," Larry said, grabbing his phone off the center column and unlocking it. The wallpaper on Larry's phone was a picture of him and his mother standing outside their church the day before his high school graduation. Eight months after that picture was taken, Larry's mother died of a sudden stroke. These days Larry still visits his mother's grave every week. At the end of each visit, he starts crying: first, over the heartbreaking loss of his mother, and then, over the terrifying loss of his own life that will occur sometime in the future.

Larry opened the internet browser on his phone and brought up the homepage of his cryonics lab. Just then a deer scampered into the road.

"Yo, look out for the—" Bart yelled.

Before Larry could react, Bart grabbed the steering wheel and wrenched it to the right. Larry slammed on the brakes. The tires screamed on the pavement. Startled by this sound, the deer stopped in the middle of the road and looked at them. As Larry fumbled for a grip on the steering wheel, his phone squirted out of his hand and clattered across the dashboard. Then the car slid into the right lane and screeched to a lurching stop less than a foot from the deer's body. The deer stared at

Larry and Bart for a long moment and clopped away across the pavement.

"Holy shit," Larry said.

"Wow," Bart said.

"You alright?"

"Yeah," Bart said. He took a deep breath and let it out slowly. "You?"

"Yeah," Larry said, nodding. "Now you see why I want to upload my consciousness into a computer."

"Yeah, seriously," Bart said. "No deer inside a computer."

"I was actually talking about the randomness and fragility of an organic life existing within an indifferent universe, but sure. I guess that works too."

"Oh," Bart said. "But what about computer viruses?"

Larry scoffed and started turning the steering wheel.

"Fuck you," Larry said, with a good-natured laugh.

"Hey, I'm just trying to help you achieve your grand dream of living until the heat death of—" Bart said, but then a black Range Rover came up from behind and leaned on its horn for six long seconds.

Both men turned around and looked at the Range Rover.

"Alright, alright, just go around, Jesus," Larry said. Icy air rushed into the car as Larry stuck his hand out the window and waved the Range Rover on. Once it was gone, he grabbed his phone off the dashboard, turned up the heater, and pressed his foot to the gas.

Doug's Food/Mood Journal, Day 1 - 12/31/12 - AKA: LAST DAY OF FATASSERY

7:30 a.m.:
1) Half package of Mallowmars, three weeks expired.

Verdict: white spots on chocolate, cookie plate dry and chewy, outer layer of marshmallow filling hardened into fibrous, crust-type thing. Definitely expired, but still very tasty. Maybe even better than normal. Should think about writing email to Mallowmar people about idea for new, tougher texture of marshmallow filling. Could take off. Ha. Could skyrocket this chump into big leagues of cookie R and D. Ha. Could be start of new career as food scientist developing cutting- edge cookie designs for world of tomorrow. Ha. Could be key to winning back Lindsay. Ha, ha, ha. Sure thing. Keep dreaming, chump.

480 CALORIES, 20 g FAT, 48 g SUGAR

2) One and one half big cups, choco milk (normal purple cup from kitchen, estimated size: 16 oz).
Procedure: syrup in cup, milk filled to top, thirty Mississippi's of careful but vigorous stirring with large spoon that reaches bottom of cup, drained halfway, syrup in cup, refilled to top, twenty Mississippi's of blah blah stirring, drained to bottom, cup held over mouth so thick strings of remaining syrup can sloooowly drip (the glorious waiting!) down onto outstretched tongue.

MUST REMEMBER: Lindsay hates "gross" displays of fatassery, so can't do stuff like that starting tomorrow. No licking plates clean either. Can't take any chances. Have to get her back. Have to stay disciplined. Also, should check internet job boards again to see if new positions (ha) have been posted since last week. Have to prove to her that this chump can stand on own two legs. Should not expect diet-improvement methods documented in food/mood journal to be enough. Must knock her socks off with impressive (but survivable!) job as well.

Breakdown: 24 oz 2% milk, six tbsp Nestle Nesquik choco syrup.

Verdict: nice uniform syrup blend, beautiful ebony coloring, buttery yet clean mouth texture, near-optimal thickness of froth on surface of milk. Very thirst-quenching. Almost no stickiness left on tongue after each sip. Also acts as perfect complement to stale Mallowmars, with choco creaminess of milk softening crusty outer layer of marshmallow filling. Great combo. Should try to get Lindsay to try once she comes back. Maybe then she'll understand how hard it can be to say no to something good when everything else feels so bad.

720 CALORIES, 15 g FAT, 105 g SUGAR

8:25 a.m.:

1) Two 17 oz bottles of water, Poland Spring.

Verdict: crisp, clean, and almost creamy smooth, with sweet, apple-tinged finish. Don't understand how some people say water has no taste. Each time this chump cracks open bottle and takes sip, he can almost always taste some difference between Poland Spring, Dasani, Aquafina, and Value King store brand. Not sure about Shoprite brand because never tried, but that one probably has own taste too. Probably from different minerals present in water blend. Interesting thought, though. Maybe this chump's biggest talent is super-powerful taste? Therapist Emma always says to utilize every skill you have, no matter how silly or useless it seems, but never says how. If super-powerful taste is silly skill this chump has, how can that be used for job or career? How do weird old guys with gold-plated spoons get jobs as professional ice cream tasters? Where do they even start in order to get on correct path that will lead there? Been looking at internet job boards since breakfast and haven't seen postings for anything like that. Only saw warehouse and janitor jobs, but won't be doing that again, not after humiliating disaster at Harrison's with mixed-up orders. Have to remember to look up dyslexia later. Maybe that's why numbers kept getting transposed? Either way, can't let that happen again. Never, never, never want to feel that awful feeling again. Will work like heck to make sure things are different for lucky number thirteen next year. Fatassery, Lindsay-less life, and lonely sadness not only things ending tomorrow. So is unemployment and terrible fear of getting yelled at by boss.

0 CALORIES, 0 g FAT, 0 g SUGAR, 34 oz WATER CONSUMED

<u>11:30 a.m.:</u>

1) BIG SALAD

Breakdown: ENTIRE 10 oz container of Dole 50/50 spring mix and baby spinach salad blend, four oz baby carrots, three tbsp parmesan cheese, three oz balsamic vinegar, two tbsp crushed red pepper.

Procedure: wanted to try something different here. Thought more about writings in last entry and decided to get head start on better eating. Because why wait until tomorrow? Why not start now? Also, was starting to get jumpy, so had to distract brain with something. Was at risk of checking Lindsay's profile again, even after vow to not do that, so took quick drive to Value King and bought salad stuff. Closed eyes while walking past candy and chip and pizza and cookie and ice cream sections and then went straight to vegetable area and bought above stuff. Looked up at ceiling while in checkout line and almost poked lady in eye when handing over money, but got out of there without caving.

Verdict: spring mix in good shape right out of container, not too wet or gross, nice crunchy texture, but then started eating and almost gagged from terrible taste and awful squeaking sound of greens rubbing against teeth. Also, didn't add enough cheese to cut acid sharpness of balsamic, so vinegar taste very strong and overpowering. Felt like cheating to add more cheese, so ate rest of salad in then-current state of severe cheese deficiency. Not good. Was very aware of outside world and past sadness while eating. Not sure how to survive rest of crappy life without beautiful escape of good food, but will try. As long as Lindsay is there at table during bad meals, everything will work out. Can do anything with her help. Have to get her back.

205 CALORIES, 5 g FAT, 10 g SUGAR

4:36 p.m.:

1) Four large pieces of CBR (chicken, bacon, ranch) pizza from Geno's Third on Cambrian in town.

IMPORTANT NOTE: does NOT count against new, earlier start for healthy eating, because CBR only well-earned reward for today's hard work. Spent entire afternoon filling out two very promising job apps, and didn't check Lindsay's profile once while working. Also, ate entire gross salad (without adding extra cheese!), so actually did THREE really big good things, all before timer for changing crappy life even officially started.

Verdict: simply magnificent. Made all bad things melt away for first time today. Dough chewy but firm, not soggy and wet like frozen pizza, and not stone-hard and crunchy like some pizza places around here that try to imitate super-crunchy style of NYC. Hate that kind. Pizza should have specific mouth-texture of pizza, not burnt toast. Toppings fantastic (as always), especially fried chicken chunks, which were cut into little rectangular strips and coated with some kind of garlic-y spice. Extra spice gave chicken great tangy flavor that mixed with savory cream of ranch and meaty crunch of bacon to create complex tapestry of beautiful flavors and textures. All around wonderful treat. Nothing better in life, except time spent with Lindsay. She creates special type of feeling that can't be copied, not even by CBR. Very sad that Lindsay and CBR cannot co-exist in new life of normal-sized assery, but easy choice to pick Lindsay.

MUST REMEMBER: have to start writing email to Lindsay later today. Do not ever want to think about that awful night again, but can't procrastinate any longer. Must finally give her rational explanation for previous actions. She deserves to know anyway. If not, very unlikely she will even acknowledge huge efforts made to stand on own two legs. So must address past issue first. Also, will need extra time for Therapist Emma to check email before sending, so must finish writing by tomorrow night.

ESTIMATED TOTALS: 2400 CALORIES, 80 g FAT, 45 g SUGAR

5:21 p.m.:

STATUS UPDATE: while driving home from Geno's, had to recline seat backward because stomach very full of chewed CBR. Not great feeling. Brought back unpleasant memories of worst days of fatassery from years past. Once back home, had to stay standing for half hour to keep pressure off bulging stomach. Finally sat down ten mins ago, but can now feel thick layer of dry-mouth stickiness starting to coat body of tongue and inside of mouth. Beginning to regret CBR indulgence already. Very mad at crafty brain for tricking chump into thinking he deserved reward of CBR for single afternoon of "hard work," because, if being honest, not much work got done in hours after big salad. Filled out one very promising job app to become jeweler's apprentice (exciting), but other job located 2000 miles away in California and never going to happen. Only used as mindless busywork to prevent crafty brain from finding justifiable excuse to check Lindsay's profile. Also, second app only took ten mins. Spent next two hours browsing Amazon and watching Mario 64 speedrun on YouTube. Can't give up though. Have to keep working. Must be better than before.

SIDE NOTE: starting to feel very scared of what Lindsay will think while reading email on Thursday night. Very painful to remember how mad she was when she left last time, but can't blame her. She wasn't meant to see what she saw that night. No one but unlucky cops called by neighbors were meant to see. Had made that clear in instructions left on kitchen table. But those thoughts gone now. Will learn to stand on own two legs instead of giving up and choosing bad alternative, like last time.

10:37 p.m.:

1) Eight peanut butter and jelly sandwiches.

Breakdown: sixteen pieces whole wheat bread, six oz Smuckers concord grape jelly, eight oz Jif creamy peanut butter, six tbsp Nestle Nesquik choco syrup.

Verdict: no more lies or omissions. Above info 100% correct. Felt very, very sad/horrible after looking at certain thing not supposed to look at, so turned back to delicious food to try to make sadness melt away. Started by making first three sandwiches with peanut butter and choco syrup. Good idea in head, but not great in RL. Sticky + sticky + dry bread + dry mouth = awful. Also, choco syrup kept oozing out between gaps in bread after each bite, so hands and face quickly became very messy and gross. Soon after that felt terrible pain in abdomen from buildup of high- pressure gas. Tried anti-gas pills, but pills just sat totally intact on top of giant mound of undigested food inside super-full stomach. From here started to worry that stomach would rip open from huge mass of stuff jammed down throat in such short amount of time. Didn't want stomach to rip open, but if being honest, would probably be for best. Not sure what good can be done with rest of crappy life even after horrendous pain of next twelve hours ends, so maybe ripped-open stomach is perfect punishment for living gluttonous life of weakness and fatassery.

3330 CALORIES, 128 g FAT, 197 g SUGAR

2) Fridge grazing.

Breakdown: two leftover meatballs, smeared with stick of butter; seven pieces pepper jack cheese, rolled into hollow cylinder, filled with ranch dressing; four partially-frozen French toast sticks, spread with butter, drizzled with extra-virgin olive oil.

Verdict: mind in very bad place here. Did not want to stop going, no matter how gross or painful. While chewing sludgy meatballs, soft chunks of butter slid down throat and almost triggered gag reflex three times. Very unpleasant feeling. Soon moved on to pepper jack, but ranch-filled cheese even worse than cold meatballs. From here had to switch back to sweet side in order to keep going, so put French toast sticks in toaster to warm up. Tried to trudge to bathroom to pee while sticks heating in toaster, but sad thoughts rushed back instantly, so had to take sticks out after less than one min. Once out of toaster, sticks felt wet and soggy on outside and hard and frozen on inside. Didn't care. Still didn't want to stop. So put butter and oil on and started chomping away. With first bite, teeth crunched through solid bar of ice while gross slurry of oil and soggy batter swirled around inside mouth like raw sewage. Probably worst thing ever tasted, but kept going and repeated procedure with next three sticks. Was terrified that pain of very sad thing and very scary future would rush back in once jaws stopped moving. Was correct.

ESTIMATED TOTALS: 2000 CALORIES, 90 g FAT, 70 g SUGAR

Report Card, 12/31/12:

Will not add up consumption totals for entire day because too afraid of number that will result. Don't want to know anyway. Won't change anything. Also, still feeling very sick from final phase, so can't go to sleep for long while. Must wait another few hours and at least one quality bathroom session before sleep even possible. Finally have extra time now to think about past mistakes, but would rather forget every single thing ever done in crappy life.

FINAL NOTE: Just after midnight, walked into pitch-dark TV room and stood in silent black for long time. Soon felt numbing wave of sour cold dripping from head to foot, draining all strength from body. Started to feel very weak, as if body would crumple into heap on floor at any moment, but legs held strong for some reason. Thighs burned, calves quivered, feet ached, and still: solid. From here everything in brain screamed in loud voices about giving up and lying down for good, but decided not to listen this time. Decided to stay standing. Felt meaningful at first, but not sure about anything anymore. Probably not important.

The Guy Who Always Felt Like He Was About to Throw Up

During college I worked at CVS with a guy named Joe who always felt like he was about to throw up. Since he was too scared to go to the doctor to get himself checked out, Joe worked each shift with a nauseous grimace plastered to his thin face, with rivulets of shiny sweat scudding down his chalk-white forehead.

Whenever a customer told him he'd feel better if he stuck a finger down his throat and got it over with, he always had the same response:

"I know it's not a very manly thing to say, but I'm too afraid to do that. I haven't thrown up in almost fourteen years, and I still remember how terrible it is."

A few days before my final shift at the store, Joe walked into the break room and asked me for a favor. Fat tears quivered in the corners of his red eyes, and his face was the same color as the blank white wall behind him.

"I can't do this anymore, Robbie," Joe said, his voice pinched and thin, his hands resting lightly on his stomach, his upper body hunched into a shape that reminded me of the number six. "I'd rather drop dead than feel like this for another minute. I'm twenty-seven years old for fucks sake, and I've lived half my life cowering in fear of this shit." He pointed to his stomach with both hands. "It has to end. I can't do it anymore. I need you to punch me in the stomach as hard as you can."

In the four years I'd been here, I'd seen first-hand what a stand-up guy Joe was. He always covered my shifts whenever I got drunk the night before work and had to call out, and he always went the extra mile to help every single customer, even the really obnoxious ones who demanded to talk to the manager over an expired thirty-five-cent coupon. On top of that, he never missed work himself, despite his mysterious condition.

So I agreed to help him out. It was the least I could do for a good friend who'd covered my ass dozens of times in the past.

Since we still had another fifteen minutes left in our break, me and Joe went into the employee bathroom, propped open the door of the handicap stall, and lifted the toilet seat. Joe stood beside the toilet and closed his eyes. Though he had promised to keep his hands in his pockets during the punch, they quickly crept up his torso and settled at the base of his throat, as if anticipating the unpleasantness to come. With my back to the wall, I drew in a slow breath and smelled the astringent bite of fresh bleach, the earthy memory of old farts.

"You ready?" I said.

Joe swallowed hard and gave me a slight nod.

"Okay. You got this, man," I said. "This shit has nothing on you. Just think of how great you're going to feel when it's finally over."

I set my feet shoulder-width apart and raised my hands to my chin. Sensing my movement, Joe's face crunched into a terrified scowl. His body began to tremble.

"Three," I said, lowering my right fist and rotating at the hips. "Two—"

"Stop, stop!" Joe said, his body curling away from me like a strip of paper being eaten by a flame. "Jesus Christ! Goddamnit! I can't do it. I'm so sorry man, but I can't do it. I don't care if I have to feel like this for the rest of my life, I just— fuck. I give up. I'm sorry, man. It's too much for me. I just can't do it."

Joe sat down on the cold tile floor and rested the back of his head against the metal partition of the stall. Neither of us said anything for a while. Then I checked the time on my phone and showed it to him. We had two minutes left in our break.

"Well, you were right about one thing," he said, tearing off a long tongue of toilet paper and dabbing the sweat from his forehead. "Somehow I actually do feel a little bit better about everything now. So thanks a lot for helping me out with this, Robbie. You're a good dude. This place is going to be pretty boring without you."

"Thanks, man," I said, offering him my hand. "I can't say I'm going to miss this place, but it does suck that we won't get to hangout anymore."

"Yeah," he said, grabbing my hand and carefully pulling himself to his feet with a groan. "But it is what it is. You're graduating in what, three days? I can't expect you to keep working here after that."

"Yeah."

After a short silence, Joe thumped me on the shoulder with his sweaty hand. "Alright, let's get out of here."

A QUICK PRIMER ON WALLOWING IN DESPAIR

He mopped his milk-white forehead one last time and dropped the fat ball of toilet paper into the toilet. Then he stepped back and kicked the silver handle behind the bowl. The water roared into the pipe and sucked the floating ball away.

Who Cares What Psychiatrists Write on Walls?

Who cares what psychiatrists write on walls? is the answer I get, but it has nothing to do with my question. This is how things have been going ever since Trevor came back from Europe. I crack the silence with a question, he responds with nonsense, I get desperate and frustrated, he punishes me for smothering him.

For an hour we've been sitting in my mom's station wagon in the rear parking lot of Wendy's, watching cars pull up to the drive-thru window. But instead of giving me a straight answer or looking me in the eyes for the first time tonight, Trevor stares at the suped-up Volkswagen hatchback clogging the line at the drive-thru. It's got fancy chrome rims, tinted windows that gleam like obsidian, and other expensive-looking enhancements I know nothing about. I don't give a shit about cars. Neither does Trevor.

I'm ninety-eight percent sure Trevor slept with other women in Europe. That I can live with. Everyone goes to Europe to fuck. But what else did he do? Did he drop ecstasy and dance to hard house with a group of German architecture students? Did he vomit half-chewed haggis onto a thick oak table in a Scottish pub? This is what I need to know. Is that so much to ask? It's the stories that keep a relationship alive, not the fucking.

A short guy gets out of the fancy Volkswagen and walks up to the drive-thru window. The employee working the drive-thru screams at him and stabs her finger at his car. The guy says something back, and then he does a wavy thing with his hands next to his driver's side window. Someone in the drive-thru line leans on their horn for seven seconds. When the horn goes silent, Trevor pops open his door.

"This might get ugly," Trevor says. "I'd better see what's going on."

With the door open, my nose fills with the smells of car exhaust and grilled chicken sandwiches. It reminds me of the summer days from my childhood before my dad left, when I used to ride in his UPS van and eat fast food with him during his lunch break. Thinking back, I realize this is my only remaining memory of him where he's not leaving me behind to go somewhere else.

I unbuckle my seatbelt with a click and reach for the

door handle, but Trevor stops me.

"No, Lindsay," he says, still staring at the fancy Volkswagen. "You need to stay here. I'll handle this."

Before I can respond, Trevor plunks the door closed and slinks across the parking lot. His stride is slower and more relaxed than it was last month when I dropped him off at the airport to meet up with his friends. Does that mean something? Does anything he says mean anything?

It's almost midnight. I squeeze the steering wheel until my fingers ache. For a moment I'm overcome with the powerful desire to drive away and leave Trevor behind for good, but I can't do it. I guess it's not as easy as my dad made it look.

Trevor ambles up to the drive-thru window and greets the arguing pair with a raised hand. As I slump back in my seat and watch, my stomach grumbles. So I take out my phone and text Trevor my order of a spicy chicken sandwich and medium fries. Then I slip my phone back in my pocket because I'm not dumb enough to wait for a response.

Hercules in Upstate New York

Underneath an early May sunset of fiery pink and chalky orange, Ed Nash climbed out of the driver's seat of the sprinters' team minivan. For the past two hours Nash had been driving half of the Topine Community College Outdoor Track and Field Team up here to Barrier, NY, the site of this year's NJCAA Division III Outdoor Track and Field Championships, and for nearly every minute of that two-hour drive, his bad Achilles had been burning.

Nash pressed the ball of his right foot against the rented van's tire and stretched his Achilles. As an acidic burn sizzled just above his heel, the fruity, rotten smell of a dead animal entered his nose. But when he looked around for the source, all he saw was a few glinting cars sitting in the hotel parking lot, a wall of oaks and elms lining the pavement, and the distance team minivan parked a few feet away.

The back door of the sprinters' van slid open and someone thumped Nash hard on the shoulder. The shock of this blow bolted down the side of his body and crackled painfully in his bad Achilles.

"Having a little trouble there, Coach?" said Jumps Gomez, Nash's best long jumper, and one of two athletes from the team who had qualified to compete in this weekend's meet. Last year, when Nash was still a student at Topine CC and a hurdler on the track team, he had roomed with Gomez in a two-bedroom, off-campus apartment on Cambrian Heights.

Gomez dug his thick fingers into the shelf of muscle between Nash's neck and shoulder and started kneading the tight flesh there.

"Hey, you better watch it there, Jumps," Nash said, swiveling his head around to grin at the towering sophomore. "You act like you don't remember, but I was setting records at this meet back when you were nothing but a wee little freshman."

Gomez crushed Nash's shoulder and thumped him on the back once more before moving on and circling around to the front of the van.

"That's pretty nuts, Coach," Gomez said, as he took off his giant, earmuff-sized headphones and pressed the stop button on his old-school Sony Discman. Watching this, Nash remembered that Gomez was the only person Nash had ever met who still used a Discman and CDs in the year 2018. Gomez looked up at the Holiday Inn the team would be staying at for the next two nights. "I never knew they had a record for most injuries in a single race. You probably got that one locked up for life, right?"

"Yeah, you got jokes, huh?" Nash said. He removed his foot from the tire with a wince of pain; his Achilles burned so bad he could barely stand. Up until the end of last summer, Nash and Gomez had been best friends as well as roommates. But once Nash tore his Achilles for the second time in two years, he gave up on hurdling for good. Soon after that he graduated from Topine CC with his associate's in exercise science and moved out of the Cambrian Heights apartment. But since he didn't have the money to transfer to a four-year school to finish his degree, Nash accepted Coach Miller's offer to return to the Topine CC track team as the coach of the sprints and jumps team. These days Nash and Gomez still saw each other multiple times per week, but something in their friendship had changed. To Gomez, Nash was no longer Nash. Now he was Coach. Or at least that's how it felt from Nash's side of things. "How bout we save the jokes until you set a new record of your own this weekend in the long jump? Seven point four- nine meters, baby!"

Gomez scoffed and shook his head.

"I think that Achilles is the least of your problems, Coach, because I told you just before we pulled in here that the record is seven sixty-nine. And besides, my PR is six ninety-two, so I don't think we have to worry about good old Jumps setting any new records this year."

Feeling his face flush red with embarrassment, Nash waved Gomez off and turned around to check on the rest of his sprinters climbing out of the back of the van.

"Whatever you say, Jumps, but I still think you've got a good shot at medaling this weekend," Nash said. But as this statement passed his lips, he realized he neither believed it, nor knew if it was possible, nor cared whether it would happen or not. Since deciding last night that this was going to be his first and last trip to nationals as a coach, he didn't really care about this weekend anymore.

Moments later, as he watched Coach Miller and the distance team climb out of their van with backpacks and gym bags slung over their shoulders, Nash heard the trilling screech of a wild animal coming from the woods on his left. Before he could turn around, a skinny miler from the distance team named Mark Lombardi pointed in Nash's direction.

"Oh hey, is that a turkey vulture?" Lombardi said.

Nash turned around just as the five-foot wingspan of a black-feathered bird opened behind Gomez's knees. An instant later the bird was in flight, its black wings flapping and shuddering, its red talons swiping at Gomez from above.

"Jesus!" Nash said. He tried to run to Gomez to help, but his bad Achilles roared in pain and his right leg caved underneath him, so he crumpled to his knees beside the van and flailed his arms at his sprinters. "Get back in the van! Get in there and close the door!"

With his Achilles on fire and a sour tear of pain collecting in the corner of each eye, Nash clambered back into the driver's seat of the rented minivan. Once there he honked the horn and watched as Gomez crouched into a squat and slipped his Jansport backpack over his shaved head to shield himself from the bird's attack. Nash felt guilty and useless as the bird squawked and slashed at his friend's backpack, but the attack ended when the bird grabbed Gomez's backpack in its talons, carried the bag a few feet through the air, dropped it on the pavement, and flew away over the trees.

The instant the bird was gone, Nash and the rest of the team rushed over to check on Gomez. Jumps lay on his back in front of the team minivan, staring up at the purple sky. He didn't have a scratch on him. Scattered on the pavement around him was a leather wallet of CDs, a pair of spiral-bound notebooks, a half-eaten package of strawberry Twizzlers, his scratched-up Sony Discman, and an old Dell laptop.

While Nash checked on Gomez, Jermaine Lewis and the rest of the sprinters collected the spilled contents of Gomez's backpack. Here Nash noticed the rotting carcass of a dead opossum laying in the grass five feet from where Gomez had been standing. On the back of his tongue he tasted the horrible smell of sunbaked animal flesh.

"That bird is an asshole," Gomez said.

"Yeah. He probably thought you were trying to steal his dinner over there," Nash said, gesturing at the carcass with his head.

Gomez sat up and looked over at the carcass. A ring of black flies buzzed drunkenly above the dead opossum.

"I was wondering what that smell was," Gomez said, as he stood up and walked over to the front of the van and picked up his leather wallet of CDs and zipped it up with three quick zings. "For a minute there I thought you forgot to put on deodorant again, Coach."

"Yeah, yeah, keep talking, Jumps," Nash said. He tried to force a good-natured smile onto his face to show that he was still one of the guys and could handle the ribbing, but he was burned out from the drive and sick of the constant insults, so nothing came. "Keep talking."

His last weekend as a coach had barely even started, and already he couldn't wait for it to be over.

#

An hour later, while sitting on the end of his bed in the hotel room he'd be sharing with Coach Miller for the next two nights, Nash received a series of frantic texts from Jumps Gomez.

> big problem, coach!
> i need your help STAT!
> im in deep shit buddy...plz come to my room ASAP!
> that asshole bird fucked everything up!

Nash stepped into Gomez's hotel room a few minutes later. Jumps was rooming with Jermaine Lewis for the weekend, but Lewis was off somewhere else. His gym bag sitting at the foot of the bed closest to the door was the only clue he'd ever been here.

Gomez's side of the room was a mess. The sheets and blankets had been stripped off the bed and thrown to the floor; an armchair near the window lay sprawled on its side; the contents of Gomez's backpack sat piled on the floor in front of the TV.

After taking all this in, Nash turned to Gomez and asked him what the problem was.

"Hercules is missing, Coach!" Jumps said. "I called the front desk five times already, and they can't find it anywhere! That asshole bird stole my DVD!"

"Whoa, okay, just calm down," Nash said, resting his hand on Gomez's shoulder. "Just relax and tell me what's happening."

Gomez threw off Nash's hand with an angry flick of his shoulders and gestured at the floor, where his leather wallet of CDs lay open.

"My DVD is gone. *Hercules in New York* is gone," Gomez said.

"What's *Hercules in New York*?"

"Jesus Ed, you forgot already?" Gomez said. "*Hercules in New York* is my favorite movie of all time. Arnold Strong and Arnold Stang goofing it up in the city, doing long jumps at the park, flipping taxis and shit? Come on. We watched that movie a hundred times at our place last year."

Hearing this description, a faint glimmer of memory flickered in Nash's head. He vaguely remembered toiling through a train wreck of an old Schwarzenegger movie while Gomez laughed his ass off at the other end of the couch.

"Wait, is that the one from the seventies with Schwarzenegger?"

"Yeah! Jesus man, how could you forget *Hercules in New York*? That movie is comedy gold. It's one of the best ever."

Though he greatly disagreed, Nash let this comment pass without argument. "Okay, yeah, I remember. So what's the problem?"

"The problem is that it's gone! That asshole bird stole my DVD! And I can't jump if I don't watch *Hercules in New York* the night before a meet. It just doesn't work. My head gets all fucked up and nervous. I just can't do it," Gomez said, staring hard at Nash, his mouth tight with fear and worry. "Please, Ed. You gotta help me find that DVD."

Nash sighed and looked around the room. He picked up Gomez's leather wallet of CDs and flipped a few pages. Brightly colored discs lay sheathed in sleeves of translucent plastic.

"And you're sure you didn't just forget it at home?"

"Yeah, I'm positive," Gomez said. "Ever since I started jumping back in middle school, I've always watched that movie every single night before a meet. I can't jump without it. So I made sure to put it in there before we left Topine. Always in the same spot. The very last sleeve on the last page."

Nash flipped to the last page of the wallet. Every sleeve was occupied except for the last one, just as Gomez had said.

Turning the wallet over, Nash saw that the back of the wallet was scratched up. A tiny stone of gravel sat lodged in the soft skin of the leather. Nash assumed it got there when the wallet slid across the parking lot following the turkey vulture's attack.

"And you said you called the front desk already?"

"Yeah, like five times. The girl said the janitor searched the entire parking lot, but it wasn't there. They're supposed to call me if they find anything, but they haven't called," Gomez said. "So we got to go out there and find it ourselves. This is my last meet on the team, Ed, and I'm going to fuck it up for everyone if I can't watch that movie tonight. The whole team came up here to watch me. I can't let them down."

Gomez sat on the floor next to his things and held his face in his hands. Nash watched him for a few seconds, half expecting him to suddenly burst into laughter and admit that the whole thing had been a prank, but that didn't happen. Instead Gomez just sat there taking slow, deep breaths.

"Okay," Nash said, slipping his phone out of his pocket. "It's nine-fifteen. Coach Miller is going to be coming around here for curfew check in fifteen minutes, so you have to stay here for the rest of the night. But I'll go down to the parking lot and look around the van. While I'm there, I'll check with the front desk again and see if anyone has found anything. But if nothing turns up, you're going to have to find a way to put this shit out of your mind and give me your best out there on the field tomorrow, you got it?"

Gomez shook his head and scoffed.

"You know, I thought you were the one person who would have my back in all this, but I guess I was wrong," Gomez said. He stood up and walked to the bathroom. "Do whatever you want, Coach. That's what you always do anyway."

#

A few minutes later, Nash unlocked the rear door of the sprinters' van and climbed inside. A canopy of dry heat hovered above the two bench seats in the back of the van. Atop this canopy sat a pungent mix of smells: stale Doritos, fresh baby powder, rank body odor, trapped farts. With his phone's flashlight bathing the interior of the van in white light, Nash began his search for the DVD. Underneath the seats he found a single black dress sock, a tangled USB cable, an open bag of Cool Ranch Doritos, seven or eight crumpled gum wrappers, and a balled- up syllabus from a Physical Geology class. While he gathered these items for disposal, Nash remembered the last words Gomez had said to him before he came down here.

Do whatever you want, Coach. That's what you always do anyway.

Nash wondered if Gomez was right. Was he really that selfish? When he moved out of the Cambrian Heights apartment last summer, had he abandoned Gomez in some way? And what about the turkey vulture attack? Did Gomez think Nash had abandoned him during that too? Did Gomez really think Nash could've helped *anyone* with the state his Achilles was in right now?

Nash moved his search outside. He lay down on the pavement and shined his light under the van. A few stones of gravel glimmered in the light, but he didn't see Gomez's DVD. Then, just to be safe, he circled the van, walked the grass near the opossum carcass, and peered into the trees. The white cone of his light revealed a cloud of buzzing mosquitos and tiny black flies, but no DVD. Walking back to the hotel he felt guilty and disappointed that nothing had turned up, but these worries quickly disappeared once he told himself there was nothing else he could do.

Then, as he passed through the refreshing column of cold air standing just inside the front door of the hotel, Nash got a series of texts from Gomez.

i just found a guy on craigslist who has a copy of Hercules in New York for sale

he lives right here in barrier and sells his old DVDs out of his house

i sent him a message and he responded in like two seconds and said that hes open till ten tonight if you got cash

his house is at 137 grimes street like two miles from here BTW

i know your going to do what you want no matter what, but i just thought i should give you a heads up about this guy

Reading Gomez's texts, Nash remembered the real reason why he had moved out of the Cambrian Heights apartment last year. It was because of shit like this. It was Gomez's moodiness, his passive aggression, his immaturity, his constant need to have someone coddle his fragile ego. Thinking about this, Nash felt even more certain about quitting the team after this meet. If he had learned anything in his first year as a coach, it was that managing difficult egos is about eighty percent of the job.

So Nash decided to buy the stupid DVD and be done with the whole thing. At the very least it'd give him a comeback the next time Gomez or someone else accused him of being too self-centered.

Nash walked out of the hotel and climbed into the sprinters' van and typed the seller's address into the GPS on his phone. Once the route was set, he thought about texting Gomez back, but he held off. He didn't have the patience to deal with any more nonsense tonight. So he dropped his phone on his lap and started the van.

#

Ten minutes later Nash parked in front of the two-story Dutch colonial located at 137 Grimes Street. It was just after 9:45 p.m. From where he sat in the van he could see the blue light of a TV flickering off the walls in one of the first-floor rooms, so he figured he had the right house.

Nash got out of the van and rang the doorbell. While he waited for the seller to answer the door, the chirps and cries of various insects filled the night air with song. Mosquitoes needled his neck, his ankles, the backs of his hands. Nash checked his phone. Five minutes had passed since he had pulled up in the van. With each passing moment he grew angrier and more impatient, so he mumbled some curse words to himself and walked across the lawn and peered in the window with the TV playing. A small wooden fold-out table stood in front of an empty couch. On top of the table sat a box of Cookie Crisp cereal and a ceramic cereal bowl with a silver spoon resting inside. Then, as he started to turn around to head back to the front door, an overhead spotlight clicked on behind him.

"Put your hands in the air and turn around very slowly," a man said from behind. "I'm holding a katana and I know how to use it. If you think you have enough time to draw your gun, chamber a bullet, and shoot me before I cut you down, you're sorely mistaken."

Nash raised his hands and stepped back from the window.

"I don't have a gun or anything else," Nash said, his heart smashing in his ears. "I'm just here to buy a DVD. A friend of mine told me you sell DVDs."

"Oh snap, is that you, Ed?" the man said, his voice suddenly softening.

Surprised by his name coming out of the mouth of a stranger, Nash forgot about the man's previous threat and turned around. On the front stoop of the house stood a balding, forty-year-old man holding a katana. The man wore orange basketball shorts and a black t-shirt. An elaborate, ridiculous-looking handlebar mustache sprouted from his upper lip. The man lowered the katana and gave Nash a friendly wave. The katana's steel blade glinted in the yellow light of the spotlight.

"Yeah, I'm Ed Nash," Nash said, squinting at the man in confusion. "Sorry to bother you so late, but I—"

"Need to buy my copy of *Hercules in New York* because Jumps can't jump without it and a turkey vulture stole his?"

Hearing this, Nash scoffed and shook his head.

"Christ." Of course Gomez would spill everything to some weird-ass stranger from Craigslist.

The man smiled at Nash and waved him across the lawn.

"Come on in. I'm Henry. Jumps filled me in on the entire situation."

\#

Minutes later Nash stood in Henry's basement and waited as Henry searched for his copy of *Hercules in New York* amid six floor-to-ceiling bookcases filled with DVDs. In addition to these bookcases, the rest of the basement was filled with all kinds of nerdy merchandise: Batman action figures still in the original packaging, life-size cardboard cutouts of Luke Skywalker and Darth Vader, plastic models of the giant mechs from the anime Nash used to watch back in middle school.

"You know, Ed, I know it's none of my business, but what I'm seeing from the outside of this thing is a lack of communication," Henry said, as he crouched down to search the bottom shelf of one of the bookcases. "I think Jumps is scared. He still feels very abandoned from when you moved out of the apartment last year, and he was very hurt by your behavior during the turkey vulture incident. Now he's afraid you're going to quit coaching the team and move away and he'll never see you again. This might be his last year of eligibility for sports, but he was just telling me that he's got at least another year of gen-ed classes to take care of at Topine CC before he can even think about transferring to a four-year school, so he's afraid that you're going to leave him behind yet again. And I think it's that fear of abandonment that caused him to lash out at you at the hotel."

"Yeah, that makes sense," Nash said, checking the time on his phone. He couldn't believe he was getting lectured by this ridiculous stranger on the state of his friendship with his best friend. "How much longer do you think it's going to take to find the DVD? Because I really have to—"

"Thar she blows," Henry said, slipping a DVD case off the shelf and standing up.

Nash opened his wallet and held out a five-dollar bill, but Henry didn't take the money or even look at it.

"Have you ever seen this movie, Ed?" Henry said.

"Jesus Christ, can I just buy the goddamn thing so I can get the hell out of—"

"Okay, okay, fair enough," Henry said, taking the money and handing Nash the DVD. "Let me just say one thing. In this movie, Hercules is an immortal demigod, but he also happens to be a pompous, insufferable asshole. Near the end of the movie, he loses his immortality from a poison arrow and is nearly killed. The only reason he survives is because his father Zeus restores his immortality at the very last moment. So you know, even stubborn, immortal demigods need a little help every now and then."

Nash felt tired and impatient and pissed off. His Achilles pulsed with a sour burn. "I'll keep that in mind," Nash said. "Is that it?"

Henry cleared his throat and smiled.

"Uh, yeah, that's it. Thanks for shopping at Grimes Street DVDs."

#

By 10:15 Nash was back in Gomez's hotel room, laying on Jermaine Lewis's untouched bed. On the way over here, Nash had heard Lewis's voice through the door of Rich Tomlinson's room, but Nash didn't make a stink over Lewis being out of his room past curfew check. In fact, that was exactly what Nash had wanted. This way, Nash could sort things out with Gomez in private.

But for some reason, Gomez seemed even more moody than before. He hadn't said a word since Nash had got here, not even a thank you when Nash had handed him the DVD. Following this, Nash's face flushed red with anger and his mind filled with all the complaints and long-held resentments he wished to air with his friend, but he kept his mouth shut. Instead, he watched as Gomez lay on his bed, opened his laptop on his lap, and started the movie.

Twenty minutes later, Gomez spoke.

"So I heard you're going to be quitting the team after this meet," Gomez said, without looking away from his laptop.

"Who told you that?" Nash said.

"People."

"People like your boy Henry?"

"Not just Henry. Other people too. Guys from the team."

Nash nodded but said nothing. Then he raised his right leg and started writing the alphabet in midair with his big toe. His Achilles sizzled with hot sparks of pain.

"So is it true? You going to bail out again and move away and leave me all alone in the middle of bumblefuck Topine with nobody to hang out with?" Gomez said.

"I don't know," Nash said, speaking honestly. He winced in pain as he traced the letter W in midair. "After tonight, I feel like another year of coaching would be a walk in the park."

Gomez scoffed.

"Says the man who can't make it to the bathroom without one of them steel walkers with the tennis balls on the ends."

Nash lowered his leg and looked over at the laptop screen. In the movie, Arnold Schwarzenegger threw a javelin across a baseball field in central park.

"Yeah, yeah, keep talking, Jumps," Nash said, a wide smile forming on his face. "Keep talking."

a few of my favorite words and why i like them

1: **Cudgel** (a: because dictionary.com defines it as: "a short, thick stick used as a weapon," and that just sounds cool. b: because hercules used one made out of olivewood as his weapon of choice and hercules is pretty badass if you read the myths and stuff. c: because it's cool to see d and g hanging out so close together like that, which i feel is a rare thing these days but maybe it's not, who knows, maybe they hang out all the time.)

2: **Ingurgitate** (a: because it's totally a real word that no one even knows is real, but the second you hear it you already know what it means thanks to linguistic morphology, and thats pretty cool. b: because the sound you make when pronouncing it is kind of close to the clicky, chomping sound you make when you do the thing it means, and thats called phonesthesia, which is even more cool, but no one in the world actually gives a shit about that [or language in general anymore], which is why im still living at home with my parents at age 29 and working at cvs for 10 dollars an hour and writing dumb lists on my phone while sitting in the gross employee break room at work because i have nothing better to do due to the fact that all my friends have real jobs and wives and houses and stuff so i cant even text with them anymore about how much our minimum wage jobs suck because im the only one who still has a minimum wage job because no one cares about language anymore. actually, thats not completely true. some of that blame falls on me for choosing to study linguistics [sorry mom and dad].)

3: **Cistern** (a: because it makes me picture a huge, very old basin made out of granite or basalt and the basin/cistern is filled with pure, clear, cold water and at some point a starving guy lost in the desert stumbles upon the cistern a few minutes before his death and he is so happy to find this big stone thing filled with all this cold, pure water that he gets really excited and falls to his knees and starts crying [dry?] tears of joy, but before he has a chance to take a drink, he collapses face-down in the sand and everyone watching at home thinks the writers are going to pull some last minute twist shit like the twilight zone used to do and that the guy is going to die three feet from his salvation, but thats not what happens because a few seconds later he starts moving again and he crawls over to the cistern and dunks his head in the water and he drinks for like two minutes straight and he ends up surviving, so the real twist is that he doesnt die ironically, he just survives normally. but then the next night he does die because he is just one guy stranded in the desert and it gets really cold at night so he freezes to death all alone right next to the cistern [which may or may not be how i secretly want my own life to end, i havent decided yet]. b: because the big stone cistern from the above story was probably built by aliens [but not the same aliens who built the pyramids, those were different aliens].)

4: **Toothsome** (a: because it helps me believe there is a universe somewhere out there where my teeth are all living beings just trying to make a buck in the tooth eat tooth world of my mouth and that most of them are pretty chill guys who can hold their booze and not get all toothsy when the tongue comes to town to help the food get down to the stomach because shes just trying to do her job, you know? she doesnt need any of that shit, shes just grinding it out like the rest of us.)

5: **Foolish** (a: because it's the GOAT. b: because it has the smoothest finish in the english language. c: because it can be a sick burn when used in the right situation, much like a changeup in baseball [or as al pacino says in the devil's advocate: "they never see me coming" {*gravelly laugh*}].)

6: **Extemporaneous** (a: because it's the baddest six syllable word in the game and there aint nobody who can oh shit my break is over in like thirty seconds and it looks like joe is mobbed at the register ugh god this job sucks, somebody please save me

love,
kevin

What is it?

Andy Carr is stocking shelves at his local Value King supermarket when a forty-year-old woman taps him on the shoulder and starts yelling in his face. By the woman's word the store is out of stock of a specific brand of organic, gluten-free cookies, and apparently, Andy is the one to blame for this.

"I'm sorry about that," Andy says, as he tries, and fails, to force a polite smile onto his face.

For some reason the woman is wearing a pair of giant, bug-eye sunglasses while walking around inside the store, so the only thing Andy sees when he looks at her is the darkened reflection of his own face. From this distorted perspective, he looks to be about fifteen years older than his true age of twenty-five.

"Let me check if we have any more of those in the back," Andy says, staring into his tiny, reversed face hovering in the woman's glasses.

Moments later Andy walks through the swinging doors at the back of the store. Just before he reaches the grocery section of the stockroom, the image of his haggard face pops into his head once again. He sees his sunken cheeks, his drawn face, the fat tires of loose skin hanging beneath his eyes. With this picture in mind, he decides he's had enough of these customers, enough of this job, enough of the verbal abuse he's endured for the past five years he's worked at this store.

With that sorted out, Andy continues into the grocery section of the stockroom. Once there he picks up a 12-count case of Fig Newtons and tucks the brown box under his arm. Then he types in the code to open the back door, and calmly steps outside without telling anyone he's quitting.

#

On the way home, Andy takes a detour and drives out to the dying mall on the edge of town. Here he sits in his car at the back of the Best Buy parking lot and stares out at the gray line of the highway. For the next hour he watches the cars zooming past in the distance, their metallic bodies flashing in the sun, their sleek shapes blurred by the shimmering heat rising from the sunbaked highway.

From here Andy climbs out of his car and walks into Best Buy. In contrast to the sun scorched oven of his car, the air inside Best Buy is chilly and refreshing. After a minute in the AC, the slick sweat on his lower back starts to evaporate.

Andy browses the aisles for the next forty minutes. During this time he tries to think of a way to turn his passion for movies into a sustainable career that he can use to support himself for the next fifty years of his life, but with him stranded here in upstate New York, two thousand miles from Hollywood, nothing feasible comes to mind. So, in an attempt to ease the familiar feeling of hopelessness churning away in his stomach, he thinks about his favorite actress, Jessica Chastain, and the questions he'd most like to ask if he ever got the chance to meet her.

A few minutes later Andy comes upon a cut-out bin of clearance DVDs. Rummaging through this mess he finds a brand-new DVD of the 1997 David Fincher thriller, *The Game*. Fincher is one of Andy's favorite directors of all time, and from his research into the man's career, Andy knows that *The Game* is the movie Fincher directed between *Seven* and *Fight Club*. *The Game* also happens to be the only Fincher movie besides *Alien 3* Andy's never seen, so he brings the DVD up to the checkout and buys it for five dollars and forty-one cents.

#

For the next five days, Andy doesn't leave his apartment. Instead, he passes the time sitting on a thin feather pillow on the floor of his empty bedroom. Here he eats the stolen Fig Newtons and watches *The Game* over and over on his laptop, studying every scene.

A little after one in the afternoon on a sweaty, anonymous day later that week, Andy's favorite scene in *The Game* comes up once again. Sitting in an airport lounge, suddenly suspicious of everyone and everything around him thanks to the mysterious, real-life role- playing game he has just signed up for, Michael Douglas sees a strange man staring at him from across the room.

"May I help you?" Michael Douglas says to the man, as Andy reaches into the cardboard box on his right and takes out an unopened package of Fig Newtons.

When the man doesn't answer, Michael Douglas flashes an annoyed smile.

"What is it?" Michael Douglas says, while Andy tears open the package of Fig Newtons and mouths the words along with MD.

What is it?

"What?" MD says.

What? Andy mouths.

The staring man puts down his drink and points to a spot on his shirt.

Watching this, Andy smiles to himself and forgets about his failed life for a few moments. Then he slips a Fig Newton into his mouth and starts chewing. As the wad of fruit and cookie slides down his throat, there is a sharp, urgent knock on his bedroom door.

Startled by this sudden interruption, Andy presses the spacebar on his laptop and pauses the movie. No one should be knocking on his door right now. It's the middle of the day and both his roommates are at work. He's the only one in the apartment.

What is it? Andy mouths, silent, waiting for something to happen, for his real life to finally begin.

The ceiling crackles. His stomach bubbles. Nothing happens. His room and the apartment beyond are quiet.

Andy waits another five minutes and then continues the movie. Michael Douglas pulls a leaking pen out of his shirt pocket. Andy slides a Fig Newton into his mouth. Everything keeps going.

Confession with Father Patrick

It's Wednesday, a little after ten a.m., and I'm alone in church. I sit in the confession booth for two minutes before the priests' side door opens and someone climbs in. From the heavy huff of breath and the sharp, rasping groan that comes with the creak of the closing door, I know that my confidant today is my good friend Father Patrick. The groans are caused by his bad right knee, which he injured while snowboarding up at Kentor Mountain a little over seven years ago, just before he became a priest. I know this because we talked about it in this very booth last week while my mom thought I was looking for a job at the library across the street, the place she drops me off at every morning while on her way to work. Ever since my most recent seizure two months ago, she says she doesn't feel comfortable leaving me at home by myself.

Before Father Patrick has the chance to open the little window built into the partition wedged between us, I start talking.

"I've pulled back the curtain of death, and peered at the face of God," I say. "And I'll be honest, he's not a bad looking guy. He's no Ryan Gosling, but he's up there."

Father Patrick slides open the window and breathes a comfortable sigh.

"Gretchen, good morning. I'm glad to see you're doing well. Any word on the results of your MRI?"

"They didn't find anything. So they still have no idea why the hell this is happening to me all of a sudden, at age twenty-six. But I recently had an interesting revelation that I think you'll find fascinating."

"The fact that you think God looks like Ryan Gosling?"

"I was actually talking about the curtain of death part," I say, as my right thumb starts twitching on its own. Feeling this my mind fills with images of my body going limp, my head smashing against the dusty floor, vomit blasting from my bloody mouth. (Always it blasts, the vomit, in these terrifying daydreams of mine. Never does it leak or bubble or do anything logical.) To take my mind off these awful images, I close my eyes and picture the scene from *Crazy, Stupid, Love* with Ryan Gosling and Emma Stone, the one where it's raining outside his house. "The Ryan Gosling thing was just a joke. Though I do think that would give you guys a nice boost to your attendance numbers here, if you replaced the crucifix up there with a carving of a shirtless Ryan Gosling. If you did that you might even see me here one Saturday night during mass, instead of just my mom."

"As much as yourself and the female parishioners might enjoy that, I don't think Monsignor Hoffman would share your enthusiasm for the idea," Father Patrick says.

"Well shit," I say, purposely pushing my luck, trying to get a rise out of this man I've talked to for hours by now but have never actually seen.

"Gretchen, language, please. We've been over this."

"I mean poop. Sorry Father."

My thumb finally stops twitching, so I open my eyes. From this angle, leaning my head against the back wall of the booth, I still can't see Father Patrick. But I sense his body beside me, inches away, and this is comforting. It reminds me that I'm not alone with these constant thoughts about life and death. Out of everyone in my life right now, he's the only other person who has to think about these things on a daily basis. Everyone else—Mom, Dad, my girls Rose and Linda over at the library—they all say I'm being morbid whenever I try to talk about this stuff. Or they tell me to see a therapist. But therapy costs money, which I don't have. The church confessional with Father Patrick on the other hand, is free.

"So what did you see behind this curtain of death?" Father Patrick says, breaking the silence.

"Well, I'm eighty-five percent sure I discovered what happens when we die, and I just wanted to tell you that I think you guys are on the wrong track."

"Really. How so?"

"Based on my experiences, I think *The Sopranos* got it right. I'm pretty sure it's an instantaneous cut to black, and that's it. Because when the brain can't form a memory of something, it's as if that event never happened in the first place. I know this because that's exactly what I experience right before a seizure. According to my mom, just before I had the last seizure, I walked up a staircase, went into the bathroom, and started washing my hands, but I have no memory of doing any of that. So from my perspective, it's as if those things never happened. So I'm pretty sure that's what it's like for us at the end. Even if we suffer the most horrible pain imaginable, we won't have the ability to remember it once it's over, so it'll be as if it never happened. And I'll be honest, Father. That's a lot more comforting than the stuff you guys are peddling in here."

"Interesting. But why do you find eternal nothingness more comforting than what we do here?"

Now my heart starts blasting away in my chest, a gallop of sharp, heavy thuds that click in the back of my throat.

"Because it's the knowing that's unbearable."

Saying this I realize Father Patrick can no longer help me. Despite all he's seen, kneeling beside the beds of the dying, witnessing their final moments, it's clear the fear has not yet touched him. So I climb out of the confession booth and start walking to the exit. It seems that over the course of a few weeks I've passed through his sphere of influence, just as I passed through God's, many years ago.

Medium

Okay so who here has recently lost a spouse, or a parent, or a brother, or a sister, or a best friend, or, you know, someone very special to—oh, so a good few of you have. Okay. So I'm getting a very powerful—actually can you guys raise your hands again? And keep them up?

Okay. Who here, out of everyone with their hands up, has lost a mother or a father? Or a brother? I'm also getting a brother vibe, something from an office, a cubicle, phone—the phone was very big in this person's job, very important, always talking on the phone to, you know, clients and . .. other people who talk with the—yes, you? miss? red—no behind you, her, yes, third row, next to the woman with the—yup, red top, it looked like that sounded familiar to—I'm getting a very strong phone vibe from you. They were always on the phone, doing business, making arrangements, everything over the phone, very dedicated to their job. Finance, uh uh uh business, frequent business trips and—father. I'm hearing—he's pointing me in your direction, father, mother, fath—mother, mother? you recently lost your mother, correct? No, not you, miss, I'm talking to her right next to you. What's that? You raised your hand because *You're* her mother? Oh so then it's *your* mother I'm hearing. So it's grandma who I'm hearing. That makes a lot more sense now. *Your* mother worked over the phone. She was a . . . telephone operator, secretary, lots of correspondence over the phone. Years ago. Before she retired. And very strong. A very strong, opinionated woman, correct? Much like yourself. No, no, not—yes, I'm talking about *your* mother, your daughter's grandmother. Well if she was a very shy person then that's someone else's mother I'm—who here recently lost their mother? I'm getting a very strong mother feeling on this side of the—very strong-willed woman, very *loud,* which I can attest to since she's yelling in my ear right now, but that's okay, I don't need to hear out of that ear anyway, I don't—yes! In the back, you recently lost your mother. Yes, yup, I'm getting that on my end too, always on the phone, doing business with—yes, her girlfriends, charity events, fundraisers, very active in the community, and . . . the knee. Knee problem later in life, arthritis of the knee, tendonitis, right knee, right leg, various maladies on

the right side of the—yup, yup, left eye, detached retina, exactly,
that's exactly what I'm—I found her Mom, she's doing great,
doesn't look like she's a day over twenty-one, she's—you hear that
Mom? She loves you, we all—can you say that for me one more
time, hun? just so she can—as loud as you can now . . . and there
she is Mom. There she is. I found her. It's your little girl. She
loves you, and she misses you, and she's just so glad that you're—
oh! Oh honey. Oh darling, you're so sweet, you didn't have to
come all the way up here just to give me a—no, thank *you* so
much, thank you for letting me—oh honey, I—you're welcome,
sweetie, I love you too, darling, you're so—thank you, thank you,
baby. I'm just so thankful I can use my abilities to help a
wonderful person such as yourself to—excuse me, sir, sir—yes,
you in the, no *sir*, yes you, with the phone, you're not allowed to
film this. You're not allowed to—no, no, no, excuse me, if you
would just—no, absolutely not, you are *not* allowed to film this,
and yes we did notify you about that, it was printed in black and
white at the bottom of the release form you signed before being
let into this auditorium at the beginning of the—well that's simply
not possible because my security wouldn't—no, no, that's not—
no, Victor and his team would never let anyone inside if they
didn't sign the—okay, okay, that's enough, thank you for the
enlightening—Vic can you get this guy out of—excuse me? Not
that it's any of your concern, but I need the release form for my
own safety, okay? For my own financial and legal safety. Because
without it, I wouldn't be able to do what I do. Without that, I
wouldn't be able to—okay well, you can stop right there now. You
think this is the first time I've been heckled? You really think
that? You really think that in seventeen years of changing lives,
and and and making connections, and reuniting grieving families
with their dearly departed that I've never—hold on, Vic, hold on.
No, you know what? You can let him keep the phone. No, I do.
I *want* him to film this. Because I'm sick and tired of being
attacked, and being vilified, and being painted as some kind of
criminal when all I'm trying to do is make a living and help
people to—no actually, *you're* the charlatan, sir. *You're* the
criminal. Because you signed a legally binding release form
which you are now breaking. Which is a crime. So actually,
you're the only one in this entire room who is breaking the law.
So now you can—what? What does that even mean? Cold
reading? Confirmation bias? So I'm reading books in the freezer

now? So I'm confirming your bias? Your bias against giving closure to all these wonderful people who're in pain, and who're grieving for the loved ones they've lost? Is that the bias you're talking about? The bias you have against seeing other people find peace in their lives? Because if *that's* the bias you're talking about, then you know what? I guess I am guilty. Because if you're so bitter, and so . . . angry about your own failures and shortcomings that you feel the need to come here and harass me, well then—oh, Mary mother of God. Listen up, jackass, I don't have to prove anything to you. Okay? There's a reason that I'm up here and you're down there, understand? And it's got nothing to do with spirits or ghosts or magic or anything else like that. Okay? It's called hard work. And that's something you clearly don't know anything about, since you're here with a a a video . . . . recorder trying to destroy me instead of doing something on your own. *Hard work.* That's what got me here. Nothing else. Now do you know what it feels like to be a twenty-two-year-old girl, living on her own on Long Island, two kids to feed, no job, no high school diploma, no college degree, no boyfriend or husband to help out, with thirty-seven dollars in the bank? Hmm? Can you even fathom what it's like to find yourself in a situation like that? Crunching on blocks of dry ramen noodles each night for dinner because you can't afford a pot to boil them in? No. Of course you can't. There's no way you could even imagine what that's like. And you want to know how I got myself out of that situation? You want to—oh screw you. Con artist. *You're* the goddamn con artist. You're the thief. I got myself out of that situation with *hard goddamn work.* That's how. I spent *years* talking to people, watching them, studying them, observing the tiny intricacies of facial expressions and body language, tone of voice, all of that stuff, in order to better understand, you know, uh uh uh their uh . . . similarities with their dearly departed loved ones who I come into contact with on a—you know what? You can get the hell out of here now. I don't need to explain myself to a parasite like you. Vic can you—yeah, yeah, whatever you say, jackass, I'm a parasite, you're a parasite, we're all parasites, let's do the hokey pokey. Thanks so much for coming out tonight. Drive safe now. Really, I mean that. Because that's the last thing I need, having you coming back to haunt me. Oh my goodness. I need that like I need a hole in the head. Okay. Woo, that was fun. So. Who here has recently lost a brother or a sister? I'm feeling a strong resonance on—raise your hands now—a very strong resonance on brother. Brother, brother, anyone lose a— hands? Brother, sister—anyone? Very strong-willed, water, I'm seeing water, very athletic, very big on water, loved the water, always outdoors, lots of hiking, swimming, loved the water, lots of fishing, watersports, lakes, ponds, anyone? Brother, sister, maybe a relative . . . cousin, nephew, loved the water, always drinking water—hands? Anyone? Anyone?

Some things that happened after Derrick woke up his girlfriend at 3 a.m. to watch Too Many Cooks

- Derrick (me) felt a little less scared about the future and life in general thanks to a bunch of the little creepy appearances of the killer in the background of Too Many Cooks like when he's on the stairs in the background of the family photo near the beginning and no one notices he is there

- She (Kara, girlfriend) asked Derrick what the hell is wrong with him and how can he even watch this shit and what is he doing/why the hell is he even awake right now when they have to be up by six and have everything out of the apartment by noon and just go back to sleep, and etc. Those were some of the things she said but of course she didn't say anything about the video, which was the one fucking thing he wanted to talk about with her because if all they ever talk about is stupid pointless adult-type shit and nothing fun, then what's even the point of them being together besides the occasional bang   when   she   feels   like   it

- Derrick opened word on his laptop with the idea of writing a Rory Gilmore pro/con list on the usual subject but it was too hard to think of the pros so he started writing whatever this is instead (some kind of stupid journal?)

- It became clear to Derrick that Kara doesn't understand him and probably never will but that's fine because it's really hard for even Derrick to understand himself and why he does the things he does most of the time like when he was hanging out with Ricky and the guys two nights ago and was trying to tell that great story about that time back in June before he got fired when he was at his parents' house and the neighbors were having a BBQ next door and the people were eating hot dogs and someone dropped their hot dog and bun and everything into the grass but instead of eating it like every other dog he'd ever seen, the neighbor's dog gently picked up the hot dog and the bun and everything in his mouth and tried to give it back to the lady who had dropped it, but no one else except Derrick even saw (he was watching from the back deck of his parents' house) that this funny/beautiful/indescribable moment had even happened, a cool and probably rare thing that might never happen again because what real dog on earth is going to try to give food back to a person instead of just eating it? (no dog that he knows of) but as Derrick was trying to tell this story to Ricky and the rest of the guys no one seemed to be listening to anything he was saying, they were just playing COD and not paying attention, so without thinking Derrick kicked Ricky's dog as hard as he could for some reason and the loud yelp that the dog let out before running across the floor with its nails scraping on the wood finally got their attention but before Derrick could start telling the story again they all cursed him out and made him leave which was total bullshit because like usual the people he actually wanted to talk to about something weren't even listening to anything he was saying

- After this Derrick wondered how it was possible for him to love something or a whole category of things so much while at the same time hating them and himself with every fiber of his being like how he feels right now with dogs and people and everything else

- The next thing that happened after Too Many Cooks was that Derrick stared at the back of his girlfriend's head for a while as she laid in bed. For some reason this made him feel like he was going to burst into tears at any moment but then he turned his laptop around so the blue light of the screen shined on her hair which looked really pretty like that and this reminded him of the bad old days during his year at college when he would sit alone in his room on the weekends while everyone else was out doing stuff and he would wish so much that he could just find a girl, any girl, someone who could actually like him and who would play Mario 64 and Perfect Dark and watch Scrubs or Gilmore Girls or anime with him but now that he has one he somehow feels even more alone than ever, which Old Derrick (or should he say Young Derrick) would think is crazy and impossible and maybe it is but still, he does (feel that way)

- After this Derrick got tired of all this sappy depressed shit so he started to look for a job on Indeed but everything was commercial truck driving and shit jobs in restaurants and it all sounded so hard and like stuff he'd never be able to do for more than a week even if he was qualified (which he wasn't) so he stopped after about ten mins of searching (it was really more like three, if he's being honest) and took his laptop into the bathroom and tried to whack it but the first video on the Pornhub homepage was something incredibly gross and so messed up to the point that he does not want to even type the words to describe it here so instead he ended up sitting on the cold toilet and watching Too Many Cooks again

- And that's everything that happened

Not Really a Horseradish Person

I'm not really a horseradish person has always been one of my mom's favorite things to say. It's classic Donna. Anytime me or my older brother Lex used to do an impression of her, that's the line we'd always quote. We'd turn our noses away from the offending pile of invisible horseradish, scrunch our lips up tight as if we'd just taken a bite out of a fresh lemon, and say the line. Because if there's one thing we all know about mom, it's that she hates horseradish. Just like we all know that dad has bad gas and that Lex thinks dogs are annoying and needy. But now that I'm back home for the first time in almost two years, house sitting for my parents while they're hiking the Adirondack Trail on vacation, I'm not so sure about anything anymore.

Because stacked here in the basement, hidden behind dozens of cans of Campbell's Tomato Soup and Bush's Baked Beans, are at least twenty or thirty unopened bottles of Gold's Prepared Horseradish.

"They can't be dad's, no way, Rach, not with his stomach," I say to the empty room. Not long after I broke up with Derrick and moved back here for a month to watch the house, I got into yet another big fight with my best friend, Kristin, over how she stops talking to me every time she gets a new boyfriend. That was three weeks ago. Not surprisingly, I haven't heard from her since. A few days after that fight, while I sat drunk and depressed in the empty living room with a bottle of Pinot Grigio in my hand and an old episode of Futurama on the TV, I invented an imaginary friend to take Kristin's place. Her name is Rachel. She's twenty-four just like me, but unlike me, she's a badass who doesn't take any shit from anyone. Thanks to this and other reasons, she's quickly become the best friend I've ever had. Because apparently the secret to lifelong friendship is to create an entire person out of thin air who will never abandon you for a guy.

I look over the bottles of horseradish and then turn to the blank wall beside me, the place where Rachel would be standing if she were real.

"I don't get it. They can't be Lex's either. He's been gone longer than us."

I imagine Rachel lowering her chin and giving me a look

that says, Kara, please. *We both know whose they are.*

A stone-age cold seeps through the concrete floor and soaks into the soles of my bare feet.

"But why would mom buy all these if she hates horseradish so much?" I say, picking up one of the bottles. The bottle is cold and smooth, completely free of dust. The soft pad of my thumb sticks to the chilly glass.

Just then a raccoon peeks out from behind the castle of unused paper towels and plastic- wrapped sponges standing in the corner of the room. The raccoon lets out a loud chittering noise and darts toward my bare feet. A shrill scream leaps from my throat; my body shudders in panic. On reflex, I throw the bottle of horseradish to the floor and run out of the room. The bottle shatters on the floor. The raccoon's tiny claws skitter on the concrete. I sprint up the stairs and slam the door behind me.

Back in the kitchen, I sit at the dinner table and listen to my wheezing breath, the heavy thud of my slamming heart. Once I catch my breath, I look over at Rachel.

"This fucking house, Rach," I say. "I swear."

Instead of laughing at me or ignoring me or browsing Instagram on her phone like Kristin would do in this situation, Rachel rests a weightless hand on my shoulder and nods in understanding.

To get my mind off the raccoon, the mysterious horseradish, and the endless, empty evening sprawled out ahead of me, I tie my hair into a loose bun and pull on mom's rubber dishwashing gloves. Then I walk into the bathroom and start cleaning the shower. With the overhead fan whirring in my ears and the sharp smell of bleach slicing the inside of my nose, I scrub hard water stains from the rounded walls of the bathtub. I scrape slimy white soap scum from the grout between the wall tiles. It feels good to stress my body like this, to do something real and tactile, to accomplish something productive with a day that would've been wasted on waiting for Kristin to call.

Despite the welcome distraction of these chores, it doesn't take long for my mind to wander back to the unexplained bottles of horseradish in the basement.

"Okay," I say, dropping the scrub brush into the tub with a clatter. "This is ridiculous Rach. We're figuring this out."

Minutes later I'm standing in my parents' bedroom, sliding open the drawers of mom's cherrywood writing desk. At the bottom of the middle drawer, laying underneath a yellow legal pad, a few issues of Star Magazine, and a calculator from the 1980s with buttons the size of postage stamps, is a red-leather book with gold-edged pages. Everyone in the family knows that mom has been an avid journal writer since she was a little girl, so I know in an instant that this is mom's most recent journal.

I take a deep breath and start flipping through the pages. Each entry is marked with the date and time of the writing, and nearly every page is filled with beautiful, looping, right-leaning cursive.

Though I'm curious to dive into the mysterious world of mom's inner life, I stop myself from reading too much. Instead, I scan the pages quickly, searching for any occurrences of the word *horseradish*.

Near the top of the entry from May sixteenth, I strike gold. So I slide my eyes back to the beginning of the paragraph and start reading.

Oh Donna, Donna, Donna, you weak, silly little girl! I'm so disappointed in you! I thought we were done with this nonsense. Eight months and seventeen days of perfection gone in an instant, and for this? For a sale on HORSERADISH of all things? Oh Donna. You break my heart. Is this what our life has been reduced to? Compulsively buying one of the most repulsive concoctions on God's green earth just so we can actually feel something for once? So we can feel the thrilling rush of taking advantage of a great sale at the supermarket? This is who we've become? The woman who buys and buys and buys every useless thing she sees in order to fill the emptiness in her heart? The woman who's too afraid to pick up the phone to tell her own children how alone she feels in this—

I smack the book closed and slip it back into its drawer. My eyes start to burn. I raise a hand to rub a tear away, but then I remember about the bleach from the bathroom and stop myself.

"Wow," I say to Rachel. "Holy shit."

Laying back on the bed, I take out my phone and call mom. The call goes to voicemail. In my message, I say that I hope her and dad are staying safe and having fun. Unsure of what else to say, I tell her I love her. Then I hang up and drop my phone on the bed beside me.

Maybe you should set a reminder on your phone to

remind yourself to call her more often once they get back, Rachel says, in her silent voice. *I'm sure she'd love to hear from you more than once a year on her birthday.*

"That's a great idea."

I give Rachel a thumbs up and grab my phone off the bed. But before I can set the reminder, I remember about the raccoon and the broken bottle of horseradish in the basement. So I roll off the bed, head back into the bathroom, and snatch the four-foot scrub brush out of the tub. With Lex gone, there aren't any baseball bats or hockey sticks in the house anymore, so the scrub brush is the best I can do to defend myself against the raccoon. But it's not until I'm standing in front of the basement door, frozen in fear, that I realize Rachel will be no help for me here. So I say fuck it and I take out my phone and call Kristin. The electronic tone trills in my ear. Kristin picks up after the third ring. I take a quick breath and start talking.

Why Can't I Fall Asleep?

Just after eleven I'm on my back in bed, lights off, sleep mask on, sheet aligned with blanket aligned with comforter aligned with soft blue blanket on top, neck relaxed, hands resting on lap, entire body still, pulse throbbing between last toes on left foot, I'm not going bald, I'm not going bald, I'm not going—lower back starting to tingle, eyes fluttering behind sleep mask, deep breath in, hold for one, two, three, okay, exhale slowly, sharp crackle in ceiling, pink and brown lightning behind eyelids, palms starting to sweat, can feel lots of time passing, will not think about morning, still many hours away, will fall asleep soon, will be rested and alert for tomorrow, no need to worry, will make great impression on new boss, will not freeze up while talking to first caller, will not get dry mouth and drink too much water and exceed allotted pee breaks, will not forget words when line stops ringing, will not sit speechless in cubicle while caller yells into phone about how inconsiderate I am, about how much of a bloodsucking parasite I am, about how I'm trying to profit off the sickness and hardship of others, nope, will not mind, will not let them get to me, will calmly ask for insurance and date of birth and move on, will not let them ruin my life again, both away from them and with, sitting in my cubicle, trapped on the other side of their anger, eating their misdirected shit, nope, will not absorb it anymore, will be iron, bedrock, that stuff they coat cooking pans with to make the eggs slide off easy, I'll be that stuff, the green stuff on the bottom of that crappy pan Mom ordered off the TV for me four Christmases in a row, oh God Mom, when was the last time I called her, oh Christ, what kind of a person am I, can't remember when I last called my own mother, hands way too hot now, have to slide out from under covers, patter of animal footsteps near window, hope they don't get into the basement again, oh yeah Mom, have to remember to call her tomorrow, should tell her about my first day at the new call center, that'll cheer her up, she'll enjoy hearing about that, well hopefully but who knows, depends how she's doing, bad day or good, hope it's not a bad one, can't handle those anymore, all that misplaced anger, her confusion of past and present, her mistaking me for Sonny again, that ass, that patch of human pond scum, that little rat who screwed her over but is still somehow her favorite, that sneaky—if I'm a bad person and a bad son and a parasite then what does that make him, that snake, that thief, that serial liar who would con his own damn mother to—ha ha, would, that's a laugh, very funny, *would*, more like did, more like did and then lied about it to his brother's face, that tightly packed ball of excrement, that—where the hell is that little weasel even living these days anyway, is he still up in Maine, that coward, or is he— Jesus I'm fully awake now, Christ what a disaster, can't be thinking about this stuff right now, have to relax, have to calm down, have to clear the mind of all thoughts, all worries, all the mental garbage that prevents relaxation, have to—yes, will do that, will pick up the mantra where I left off, just need to stay focused, deep breath, hold, one, two, I'm not going bald, I'm not going bald, imagine the lake, silver blue water all around, glowing white moon shining above, the coast far away, nothing but woods and trees, a dense forest of elms lining the water, barely visible, elms and oaks and dogwoods, way off in the distance, miles and miles, just me and the canoe and no one else, floating along, me on my back in the canoe, I'm alone but not sad, not like Sunday nights, God I hate that time, hate it so much, worst part of the week by far, so depressing and lonely, so hard to keep the bad thoughts out, those dreams of running away, of escaping all this shit, of merging onto the highway and leaving it all behind, all this unhappiness and fear, all this—can't think about that now, just have to relax, clear the mind, I'm in the canoe, water bubbling below, the rest of the world quiet, huge black sky above, just me and no one else, relax, relax, legs starting to ache, feet going numb, will have to reposition soon, God I hate this, why can't I just fall asleep, been up since before seven, just go to goddamn sleep, please just let me sleep, that goddamn Sonny, I bet that little tapeworm is sleeping like a baby right now, always has, ever since we were kids, never had trouble falling asleep, that little con artist, always snoring a minute after Mom hit the lights, and there I'd be, dead awake on the top bunk, staring at those glow-in-the-dark stars, the plastic ones we stuck to the ceiling with putty, my mind racing a hundred miles per hour, thoughts flying in every direction, him snoring and sighing in his sleep, dead to the world, comfortable and content, so ridiculous and unfair, as if he had any right to sleep like that, what with the tricks he always played on our friends, and on me, and on Mom and Dad, that little bastard, oh Jesus what a disaster, what a mess, don't want to imagine how much time has passed since I got in bed, what a stupid waste, very counter-intuitive this sleep thing is, try but *don't* try to fall asleep, try too hard and you'll wake yourself up, very stupid and unfair, makes no sense, but can't think about that now, just have to relax, clear the head, remember the mantra, I'm not going bald, I'm not going bald, I'm not—will be fine tomorrow, will do good, will call Mom after, won't worry about her slipping mind, can't use that as an excuse anymore, she deserves to hear from her son, the one who actually cares about her, even if she doesn't remember me, even if she thinks I'm Sonny, can't blame her for that, it's just the disease talking, just that awful goddamn—it's not her fault, I need to be more patient with her, more patient with everyone really, maybe then I wouldn't have to deal with this three times a year, this nighttime garbage, these first-day jitters, this cold-sweat anxiety, maybe then I'd be able to hold a job for more than three months at a time, but can't think about that now, have to relax, have to clear my head, deep breath in, hold, one, two, I'm not going bald, I'm in the canoe, I'm alone, the lake is around me, I'm alone, I'm not going bald, the moon is above, the water is below, I'm alone, I'm alone, I'm alone, I'm alone, I'm alone, I'm alone, I'm alone, I'm alone, I'm alone, I'm alone, I'm—

I Found My Heel at the Foot of an Oak

I found my heel at the foot of an oak. I remember someone somewhere calling this bone a talus, or maybe it was a calcaneus, maybe that was the word they had used, but I can't remember who said that, or where I was when I heard it, or what my name was when I still had a use for this part of my body, but I know this bone was mine, that it was a part of me, that at one time I used it for something very often, maybe even every day, but that was before I got lost in these woods I've been wondering around in for a very long time. Or maybe it hasn't been that long that I've been here. I can't remember anything that feels like a yesterday or a last week. Those words don't really make much sense to me anymore because I haven't slept for a while. Or maybe I have and I just can't remember. I don't know.

This is what I do know: sometimes it's light out for a while. Then it gets dark. Then it gets light again, and bars of gold sunlight knife through the naked trees and crawl over the quilt of dead leaves on the ground. Every now and then it rains, but I don't feel anything. The water I mean. That I can't feel. And the cold, too. I never get cold anymore. But I don't know if it's because I can't feel it anymore, or if it's because these woods just don't get cold. I remember there being places like that, woods that don't ever get cold, but I don't know who told me that, or where I was when they told me. All I know is I wasn't here. Or maybe I was and I just can't remember. Maybe I've always been here.

Either way, that's everything I know. Actually that's not true. I know some other things, too. I know there are pieces of myself scattered all around here. Or at least one piece, this heel or talus or calcaneus that I just found by this oak. Or maybe this was a knee, my knee? Maybe that was the word they used to describe this thing that was once a part of me. Maybe this was my knee. Whatever it was, every now and then I find these pieces of myself on the ground, and I start remembering things that make no sense. Words, names. Places I've never been to but have somehow seen. Places that must exist somewhere outside the woods. But then I get confused or I see a new path that might lead out of the woods, and I decide to move on. There are a thousand winding paths in these woods, and one of them has to be a way out, so I've got a lot of ground to cover. There's no point in staying in one place for too long.

But this time I didn't do that. Instead, I bent down and looked closely at this piece of myself on the ground. Following this I reached out and touched it, *but no matter how much I scratch that spot on the back of my foot, it doesn't stop itching. So I slip my heel back into my shoe and straighten up in my desk and try to concentrate on Prof. Gardner's lecture. Moments later the itch gets worse, so I start tapping my heel on the tile floor. My turquoise scrubs swish with each small movement of my leg.*

Prof. Gardner stands at the front of the classroom. To her left is a white screen with a projection of a human skeleton on it.

She presses a button on her computer and advances to the next slide, which zooms in on the foot. Now she points with a yardstick at the foot and identifies the bones. Her voice is low and sharp and raspy, like the sound of someone scraping old paint off the side of a house.

She says:

tibia, talus, calcaneus;

navicularis, cuboid;

cuneiforms, there's three of these, medial, intermediate, lateral, one, two, three;

metatarsals one, two, three, four, five;

the phalanges.

She says:

These are the ones you need to know, ladies. So you should probably write this down.

The girl sitting next to me slides her toe under my tapping heel, and the sound stops. Now I hear nothing but Prof. Gardner droning on at the front of the room.

I turn my head and look at the girl sitting next to me. Her hair is tied up into a blonde ponytail and her eyes are ice blue. Her scrubs are pink. She is smiling at me, smiling in that way a person smiles when she is deeply annoyed and is trying to hide it. Then she whispers a name and some words.

Amanda, chill. Everyone's getting pissed.

With these words the itch on my heel goes away, but I know that if I sit here for another moment I'm going to scream or burst into tears or jump out the window. So I grab my things and leave the room. Moments later I'm sitting in a locked stall in the bathroom at the end of the hallway and my head is in my hands. I'm trying very hard to cry quietly so no one outside will hear, but I can't stop up the noise and it echoes loudly off the hard tile floor. Sitting here I try as hard as I can to think of a way to survive this life and this day and all the empty, pointless, identical days to come, but I can't think of anything except the bad plan, the last resort, the one that never goes away, the one that comes after one last hike in the woods out by Kentor Mountain. Now the bathroom door opens. Hearing this I press my hands over my mouth and close my eyes, but a minute passes and nothing happens, so I open my eyes and scratch the back of my foot. Looking down, I found my heel at the foot of an oak. I remember someone somewhere calling this bone a talus, or maybe it was a calcaneus, maybe that was the word they had used, but I can't remember who said that, or where I was when I heard it, or what my name was when I still had a use for this part of my body, but I know this bone was mine, that it was a part of me, that at one time I used it for something very often, maybe even every day, but that was before I got lost in these woods I've been wondering around in for a very long time. Or maybe it hasn't been that long that I've been here. I can't remember anything that feels like a yesterday or a last week. Those words don't really make much sense to me anymore because I haven't slept for a while. Or maybe I have and I just can't remember. I don't know.

Sexy Rexy's Homecoming Feast

For his fortieth birthday, Lance bought himself a red-tailed boa and named it Sexy Rexy. When he returned to his empty apartment, he masturbated to a video on Pornhub called "MASSIVELY JACKED STUD ANNIHILATES SUBMISSIVE TWINK." Then he turned off his phone and set up Sexy Rexy's living enclosure, feeding tank, and hide box. For dinner Lance ate an entire chocolate cake and washed that down with half a bottle of champagne. Then he smoked a pack of Marlboro Lights and came back inside and threw up in the bathroom for half an hour. After a long, hot shower in which he threw up one more time and sobbed for ten straight minutes, Lance fed three mice to Sexy Rexy. The salesman at the exotic pet store had warned Lance not to feed Sexy Rexy more than two mice per week. But this was a special occasion. *And besides,* Lance thought to himself, *rules are made to be broken.* Before dropping the first pre- killed mouse into Sexy Rexy's feeding tank, Lance held it by the tail and looked at its tiny legs dangling in the air. Then he named the mouse after a man he had known in the past.

He named the first mouse after the priest who got him drunk off sacramental wine at age eleven.

He named the second mouse after his father, who pushed his head through a window after walking in on him making out with the running back from the JV football team.

He named the third mouse after his college suitemate who od'd on xannys and vodka, the only man he had ever loved.

Tongue Stone

At ten years old, Scooper lived life through his mouth. For him, most things weren't real until he felt them on his tongue, awash in sticky saliva. Summer days he wandered his development alone, his cheeks fat with blocks of cheese or sugar-coated jawbreakers, with chalky pebbles from the street or spiny chips of bark, with freshly-picked leaves shaped like stars and knives and tears and eggs. It was the glide of these things in his mouth, the pungent flavors on his tongue, the clattering against his teeth, that gave life to the world.

Later that summer, on a hazy Saturday morning in August, Scooper went off to look for some new tastes in the woods behind the development. Just before noon he came upon the haunted creek the neighborhood kids always talked about. Growing up he'd heard ghost stories about a boy who had fallen into this creek and disintegrated into bloody chunks. That story had scared him when he was young, but he didn't really believe in that stuff anymore, so he felt no fear when he kneeled in the soft dirt and cupped a handful of water for a drink. As he lifted the cool liquid to his mouth, he saw something weird sitting on the bed of the glittering creek: a gray, oval-shaped stone with a neon pink stripe wrapped around the middle.

Scooper pulled the stone out of the creek. It was a little bigger than his palm and felt oily and warm near the center. When he pressed his thumbnail against the pink stripe, the shimmery material flexed. Then, while trying not to think about the missing boy and the bloody chunks, Scooper carefully broke the stone in half.

The pink stripe crackled apart with ease and flaked into brittle sheets like mica. Some of the sheets fluttered to the ground and glinted with a greasy, metallic shine. Now Scooper looked inside the stone and found a clear, trapezoidal crystal; seeing this, he couldn't control himself any longer. He dropped the stones in the water and slipped the crystal into his mouth.

The taste was glorious. Like a beam of light refracted through a prism to reveal all the colors of the rainbow, the crystal seemed to contain every flavor he'd ever tasted. It was sweet like watermelon, yet spicy like a jalapeno; it was creamy like a milkshake, yet sour like a Warhead; it was salty like a beach pebble, yet tarry like pine bark; it was bitter like an elm twig, yet savory like a mushroom. It was the entire world distilled into taste, and it was rolling on his tongue.

The crystal dissolved like a breath mint over the next thirty minutes. Once it was gone, Scooper scoured the creek for more of the special stones, but an hour of thorough searching turned up nothing. From here he decided to head back home for some lunch. He knew no other taste could ever compare with what he'd just experienced, but he didn't have much of a choice. The crystal had coated his tongue with a thick paste, and his thirst had suddenly turned savage.

Scooper trudged through the sweltering woods back toward his house. With each step, the paste on his tongue thickened: it spread down his throat and invaded his lungs. Soon fear overtook his mind and he began to run. Oaks and elms knifed past as he sliced down the trail, dodging exposed tree roots. His breath rasped painfully in his chest; a minute of running scoured his throat like a swallow of powdered glass. After a few minutes, Scooper realized he had made a mistake and had run in the wrong direction. But by now he was in too much pain to do anything, so he lay down on the trail and stared up at the diamonds of blue sky nosing through the canopy.

Scooper woke in the dirt some time later. His joints felt as stiff as solid rock. His muscles pulsed with sharp jabs of cold pain. Throbbing behind his teeth, his tongue lay cracked and huge and iron-hard; and when he tried to close his mouth, his lips wouldn't meet. It seemed that his tongue was too swollen for his mouth to close. From here Scooper began to cry. If not for his vicious thirst, he might've stayed there forever, waiting for someone to save him.

The sky was pink when he got back to the creek. Crawling through the dirt to the bubbling water, Scooper noticed that it too had turned pink. Now he looked around and saw that it was not just the water and the sky that had changed: the entire world shimmered with the same greasy pink as the stripe of the special stone.

Scooper ignored the color and leaned his stiff body over the water. Only his thirst mattered now; everything else could be sorted out later.

The tip of his tongue touched the water first. Moments later Scooper shuddered in horror as a colorless crystal slid out of his mouth and dropped into the water with a loud plop. The trapezoidal crystal sank to the bottom of the creek and tumbled along the bed like a child doing cartwheels. Feeling an alien emptiness in his mouth, Scooper realized that the crystal was his tongue, and that the story about the missing boy had been true. From here Scooper lurched into the creek in a panic and clawed along the bed for the tumbling crystal, but as the water washed over him, his skin began to dissolve into heavy gray dust. Soon the world went dark and pink sheets of mica flowed from the orbits of his skull. Muscle, sinew, brain, and bone followed in the same way as skin and eyes, and by the time the sunset blazed pink that evening, a new stone was forming under the water. Contained within were all the flavors his tongue had ever tasted.

Apartment 4 1/2 B

When James Paul graduated college on a hot, dry day in May of 2008, he realized, for the very first time in his life, that he'd been born in the wrong decade. Or at the very least, he realized he'd been born in the wrong year of that decade, because he suddenly found himself stepping out into a world of finance that had been ravaged, disemboweled, and thoroughly ripped apart by the global financial crisis of 2007. And for a young man of twenty-two who possessed an undergraduate degree in Economics but no real plans of exactly what it was he wanted to do with his life within that dizzying field of complex mathematics and endlessly swirling decimal points, the decision of what to do *after* graduation loomed more frightening and difficult than any other he'd faced before. And so maybe that was why, instead of finding a place to live in Manhattan or Brooklyn, he decided to move into the perpetually dark, one room apartment on the top floor of a grungy apartment building in his hometown of Topine, NY.

"It's just safer, it's a much safer bet, with things so unpredictable in finance right now," he said to his parents a day after the move, as he sat stiff and uncomfortable in the living room of their house, the house he grew up in, the house he used to call his own but couldn't anymore. And as he sat there, fondling and crushing the bunched seam of rough denim at the hip of his jeans, he suddenly felt like a stranger in his own life. "It's just temporary. Just until things calm down and the job market shakes out. Then I'll start looking for a place in the city, closer to . . . you know, the better jobs and everything."

The silent, slow nods of approval he received from his parents showed their satisfaction with that explanation. And it did sound like a good plan; a *smart* one even. That had always been the key word with them. So, as he explained the fabricated logic behind his decision, his voice droning reedy and dry in that newly unfamiliar room, he even started to feel some relief from the guilt that had been bubbling hot and acidic in his stomach ever since he took the coward's path and moved back home after graduation.

And it was this small success that stopped him from telling his parents about some of the more unorthodox details of his new apartment. Details that, had he shared them that day, most likely would've prompted his father to slide to the end of his chair in head-cocked alarm and command his son—in those hard short bursts of forceful consonants—to move out of that damn apartment at once. But James Paul didn't share those strange details on that day, and instead, he left his former home among beaming smiles, tight hugs, and heavy thumps on the back.

Later, as he walked home following this visit, feeling alien and strange inside his own skin, he had to admit that those bizarre aspects of his new living situation injected a sense of thrilling mystery into his drab life. Never before had he heard of an apartment building with a half floor, but now that was exactly where he lived, on the fourth and a half floor of the Tannembaum Apartment building on Grimes Street. In reality, his door only stood on a little raised landing hovering about six or seven feet above the carpet of the fourth floor hallway—a landing accessed by a short staircase at the far end of the floor—but the asymmetrical floor plan and the fascinating uniqueness of his apartment number—*apartment 4 1/2 A*—made him feel like he was living inside a surreal painting or the impossible twisting architecture of a vivid dream.

But what truly grabbed James Paul's fascination, was the apartment next door. Apartment 4 1/2 B. His sole neighbor on the fourth and a half floor. And from the moment his landlord Daniel Tannembaum had told him about that room—("Oh and by the way, nothing you have to worry about, but the place right next door to you, four and a half B, we've had it sealed off since sixty-eight . . .")—he'd found it impossible to get that mysterious, inaccessible place out of his head. And as much as he couldn't—or wouldn't—admit it to himself, he knew he'd chosen to move into that specific apartment because he couldn't imagine living his life without knowing exactly what, if anything, had been sealed away inside apartment 4 1/2 B.

A week after moving into the new apartment, James found a minimum-wage position as a teller in one of the local banks. And as he went about the mundane, brain-numbing business of his day-to-day life, the mystery of apartment 4 1/2 B was never far from his thoughts. Often, he'd find himself carrying out some mind-deadening task—listening to the crinkling, papery swish of endless twenty dollar bills passing through his hands—when another puzzling question about apartment 4 1/2 B would suddenly pop into his head:

Had Tannembaum himself ever seen what was inside apartment 4 1/2 B?

Who would design a building with such a strange, asymmetrical floor plan?

And these questions only multiplied when two weeks later, after waking up from a vivid dream at three a.m., James first noticed the smell.

It was a faint smell; the kind that floats thinly in the air and hovers just below the awareness of an active mind. But it also had a bitter, astringent bite that stung the sensitive, wet flesh lining the inside of his nose. And then there were the other smells buried within the multitudinous whole: the black, ashy notes of burning brush or sticks; the thick, suffocating tar of heavy ink and newsprint; and the round, hyper-foul sweetness of human body odor.

The next morning James couldn't stand it anymore, so he stomped down to the basement to talk to Tannembaum.

"So you've *never* been inside there yourself?" James said, standing in front of Tannembaum's desk as the huge, round man sat hunched and mumbling to himself over a messy white ocean of scattered paperwork.

"I have, Mr. Paul, and I know exactly what's in there. Nothing. I was standing three feet from the doorway of that room when my father had it sealed up in sixty-eight. So I can tell you, without a doubt, that there's nothing in there," Tannembaum said, suddenly looking up at James with a quick, jump-cut snap of his neck. The man's plump face shined with a thin glaze of sweat. Tannembaum sighed and his expression softened into the exhausted contentment of a severely overworked man who nevertheless loves his work. "Okay. Here's the story. Because of the, *artistic liberties*,"—he sighed heavily here, as if the term sickened him—"taken by the architect in the design of this building, the second room on the fourth and a half floor, apartment four and a half B, ended up with two of its walls having only about five feet of floor space between them. Five feet . . ."—he squinted his eyes and looked up at the ceiling—"three and a quarter inches if I remember correctly. And because of that, my father couldn't get a single person to rent the damn place. And so that's why he had it sealed up. So it's just easier this way. You get to enjoy a few extra square feet of space on your side, and I don't have to deal with the headache of worrying about that place on the other."

"Okay, but you just said you haven't been in there since—"

"Sixty-eight. And neither has anybody else. I promise you, there's nothing in there. And I'd show you myself, but then I'd have to get a crowbar to wedge the door open. Now," his chair let out a squeaking groan as he leaned back and let the heavy weight of his wet-cement stare once again fall onto James' shoulders. "If I do that, are *you* going to pay for my door to be fixed? Are *you* going to call the carpenter, and the locksmith, to come and put a new door on that apartment? Yes or no. I'm asking."

To this, James could do nothing but give the man a feeble shake of the head.

"Good. So why don't we let it go, and you can continue enjoying your extra footage, while I get back to work. Good? Good."

But that conversation only served to deepen James' curiosity about apartment 4 1/2 B, if now, only to prove to Tannembaum that he wasn't a monumental fool for questioning the man's awareness of his own building.

And so, from that day on, James spent the majority of his free time monitoring apartment 4 1/2 B. Most days he woke up hours earlier than he had to for work, just to sit next to the thin wall of his apartment with his soft ear crushed against the dimpled plaster, listening for sounds of life or movement inside apartment 4 1/2 B. And he even heard something on a few occasions— or at least he thought he did—but he couldn't tell what exactly it was that he had heard. One sweltering morning in July he thought he heard a wheeze or a cough, but he couldn't tell if it was actually that, or if it had been the sound of someone's TV on the fourth floor. Another time, after James woke himself up at two a.m. to listen at the wall, he thought he heard the screech of a rat and the muffled murmur of a human voice speaking very softly; but the sound had been such a brief, phantom wisp of a noise that by morning, he couldn't be sure if the whole episode had happened in reality or in a half-remembered dream.

So, as the months passed and the world economy limped toward a cautious recovery, James felt himself drifting ever further from the person he'd been just a few short months before, when he'd walked out onto the lawn of the campus soccer field and shook hands with the dean of the college. Soon he lost all interest in ever moving to the city to find a new, better job in finance. A few weeks later, he stopped going out with his brother for beers on Friday nights. And by the time he'd been living on his own for half a year, he stopped visiting his parents' house for Sunday night dinner.

Now, with his world reduced to the size of the fourth and a half floor of the Tannembaum Apartment building, he began to seriously wonder why he had ever chosen to study economics in the first place. He had always been good at math, sure, but at the same time, he had always found it to be the driest, most drab subject out of all he had been taught in school. So why then, did he ever think it was a good idea to spend the rest of his life working in a field comprised primarily of a topic that bored him out of his mind?

His question was finally answered one early morning in October. As he sat in the corner of his place, his right ear pressed to the apartment wall, a distant memory from his junior year of high school suddenly flashed in his head. Back then, the question of what to do with his life had loomed over him so heavy and frightening that he had developed the nasty habit of gnawing on his fingernails to relieve the stress. And it was on an anonymous winter night that year, as he gnawed at the wet, flaking shreds of one or another of his jagged, ruined fingernails, that he overheard his dad talking on the phone.

". . . well, they can *say* whatever they want, Mike, but even a toddler knows that money is what makes the world go round . . ."

And so after hearing his dad speak those words, James decided that, for someone who didn't really want to do *anything* with his life, money was as good of a thing as any to study. At least that way, he would always have a good job to support himself until he figured out exactly what he *really* wanted to do in life.

So with that small mystery finally solved, and with the months slipping by as anonymous and quick as streaks of rain crawling down a blurred window pane, James realized that economics was just about the last thing on Earth he wanted to spend his days worrying about. He didn't want to move to New York City. He didn't want to put on a suit every day and carry a briefcase in order to make himself feel important. And he didn't want to waste his time and energy worrying about some rich old man's liquidity. His life was here. He was living inside a grand, exciting mystery. And it *had* to be solved. So that's why, on a cold, gray day in late February, instead of going to work at the bank, James walked four blocks to Winston's hardware store on Grove Street. Once there, he bought a measuring tape, a six-inch jab saw, a crank- powered hand drill, and a pack of air-filtering face masks. If Tannembaum wouldn't let him into 4 1/2 B, he would find a way in himself.

Later that night, once the stomping noise and fluttering chatter of the fourth floor finally died to roaring silence, James pushed the skittering frame of his bed away from the thin wall his apartment shared with 4 1/2 B. Measuring the width of his shoulders with the slicing yellow tongue of the measuring tape, he traced a squat rectangle at the base of the wall. Following this, he quietly and patiently turned the crank of the hand drill and punched a series of holes through the plaster, watching, in hand-trembling glee, as a miniature mountain range of plaster-dust peaks slowly collected on the floor.

From here the rest of his night was spent sawing in slow motion, drawing the saw's curved teeth over the plaster with the speed of a glacier in order to minimize the grinding noise of his work. He made the final cut just as the gray, pre-dawn light started streaming in through the foggy window at his back. Moments after removing the white rectangle of plaster from the wall, sharp, acrid air began flowing into the room. It smelled like the interior of a junkyard car that had been burned to a mangled, black ruin. Underneath this scent floated biting notes of foul, fruity body odor. Now James slipped on an old, baggy t-shirt, a pair of worn gray gym pants, and one of the air-filtering face masks. Once ready, he pushed open the window beside his bed and drew in a deep breath of crisp February air; then he dropped to his belly and entered apartment 4 1/2 B.

The moment the crown of James' skull penetrated the threshold of 4 1/2 B, something light and plastic dropped down onto his head. Feeling this sudden touch, he squirmed and thrashed his body in a momentary panic; seconds later, once he came back into himself, he calmly swatted the object off his head. Following this it bounced off the opposite wall and came to rest in what looked like a black, cast-iron bowl sitting in the center of the narrow apartment. Looking there he saw that the object was just a bag, a plastic bag filled with strips of shredded paper. As James pulled his legs through the hole and squatted between the two close-set walls, he saw that the bag was filled with shredded money. Paper bills. A quick look around the room revealed at least a hundred more bags, some clean and professionally sealed like the one that had dropped onto his head, and some soiled and spilling open; but all were filled with shredded money or old but intact bills. From here James reached his hand into one of the open bags—a kitchen garbage bag this one seemed to be—and came up with a crinkling handful of wrinkled, pre-2000s one-dollar bills. There had to be hundreds of bills in this one bag alone. Now he noticed the walls. Near the center of the room, where the bags were stacked only knee high, the walls were scorched a deep, tarry black. Seeing this James ran a finger through the dark tongue of color and came away with a fingertip coated in thick crumbles of ash. Then he turned around and looked at the window. Broken. So now he knew how the smell was getting into his apartment. Underneath the window sat ashy handprints smeared on the sill. Now he pushed open the window and looked down the sheer face of the building. A tall, sturdy oak yawned up next to the building, its gnarled trunk standing less than ten feet from the brick facade. James looked out past the tree. The woods behind the building stretched out dense and primal for as far as he could see.

Entrance, exit, cover.

From here he turned around and looked down at the cast-iron bowl in the center of the floor. A sheet of flat, dented scrap metal that James estimated to be about two feet square sat underneath the bowl. Returning to the center of the room, he pushed the bag of shredded money out of the bowl and picked up the concave object with both hands. He braced his body for the heavy weight of cast-iron, but instead the bowl flew up in his grip with shocking ease. Cast-iron it was not, but the jarring force of this pull caused a plume of ash to puff into his face. James shielded his eyes and turned his face away from the cloud and squatted down on his haunches until the ash dissipated.

What the hell was all this?

Checking inside the bowl, he saw a charred, curled sliver of shredded money. Seeing this, he looked up at the ceiling. No smoke detector in here. Now he looked at the walls to his left and right again. The black tongues of color seemed to be darkest and most concentrated near the center of the room where the bowl had been sitting. It didn't make sense. And then it did.

"He's burning the money," James whispered out loud to himself, in a voice of hushed reverence. And then he said the same words again, but this time he said it with a nod of his masked head, with a flat tone of deep understanding. "He's burning the money." And then he said it a third time, just to solidify the realness of the idea, to preserve in his memory the otherworldly strangeness of this experience. Because suddenly, all this seemed to make more sense to James Paul than anything else had before. Nothing else seemed to match the importance, or the necessity, of the bizarre acts that had taken place in this strange, charred shrine of destruction.

James put down the bowl and stood up and walked to the sealed door. When he pushed the stacked bags of money out of the way, he saw, smeared in the black streaks of ash-slicked fingertips, a finger-stroke painting of a spinning a black hole. And underneath the black hole stood the Twin Towers of the World Trade Center: the dual, identical buildings, the narrow vertical slits of rectangular windows, the single, needle-like antenna rising from the roof of the left tower. In this strange artwork, the top of each building was being sucked into the center of the black hole.

James stared at this painting for a long time. After a while, he finally understood what he wanted—no, *needed* to do with his life. He may have been born in the wrong year of the wrong decade, and he may have rushed blindly into the wrong career, and he may have followed the coward's path in life, but none of that mattered anymore.

He now knew what to do.

He dropped to his belly and squirmed through the hole in wall. Once back in his own apartment, he grabbed his wallet off the dresser, walked into his half kitchen, and picked up the lighter with the long plastic snout he used to light the stove. Then he locked the door of his apartment and wedged the back of a chair under the knob. Moments later he squirmed through the hole in the wall, pulled the bed frame in front of the hole, and slid the square of plaster back into place.

No longer did he feel like a stranger to himself. Now he removed the mask from his face and let it fall from his hand. From here he closed his eyes and drew in a deep breath. The stench of the apartment passed through his nose, stinging and slicing all the way. Once the ashy air filled his lungs, he opened his wallet and slipped out a crisp twenty dollar bill. Moments later the bill fluttered into the charred bowl. With a click of the lighter's trigger a flame appeared, orange and shuddering, and soon the corner of the bill was on fire, the young, crackling flame slowly eating the taut paper. Not long after this he heard a sound outside; it was the oak beside the window, creaking, as if under sudden weight. Then came the hard, huffing grunt of a man, the scrabbling scrape of shoes against bark. James turned back to the bowl. By now the bill had curled and shriveled into a brittle black spiral of charred ash. A thin string of gray-black smoke rose to the ceiling. James breathed the smoke and stared at the painting on the back of the door. The room went dark as a shadow blotted out the gold sunlight of dawn leaking through the broken window. Seeing this, James Paul turned his head just as the window slid open.

Manga

This morning I stole a violin and sold it for drugs. It belonged to a blond-haired kid no older than fifteen. I took it after the kid walked out of church and started masturbating to a manga in the woods. Later, as I pushed off in the Value King bathroom down the street, I thanked God for anime tits. When I came down, I wondered why he made me.

Good Shit

Today my parents kicked me out of the house for the fourth time in a year. They said it was for good this time, but they always say that. When I talked to Father Patrick about it, he changed the subject to rehab and NA. But I still have my dad's iPad I stole and the shoelaces from his new Nike running shoes, and I can't let good shit go to waste.

Sunrise

Tonight I slept in the grass behind the church rectory. Father Patrick lets me do this sometimes as long as Monsignor Hoffman doesn't see. Under a glinting powder of summer stars, I fought the sick and cursed and cried. I shat in God's bushes and pissed on his grass. And yet, in the morning, the gold sun bathed me in warmth and light.

J.B. in the Desert

When Foreman Douglas smelled alcohol on J.B.'s breath for the third shift in a row, he fired J.B. from his new job at the oil refinery, J.B.'s fifth career in the past seven years. That night J.B. got drunk on Ironroot Corn Whiskey and reminisced about his days as a Texas Golden Gloves amateur bantamweight champion nearly twenty years ago. With the memories of his glory days flitting through his head, J.B. soon found himself darting drunkenly from one end of his trailer to the other, dodging invisible punches from phantom opponents, and trash-talking every asshole who'd ever looked at him the wrong way. Then, when the picture of Foreman Douglas's fat face suddenly appeared in his mind, J.B. stomped out his front door and started the twelve-mile walk to the oil refinery to settle things for good with that chickenshit of a man. But after lurching through the soupy darkness for nearly two hours, J.B. found himself hopelessly lost in the west Texas desert.

For the next two days J.B. trudged the rugged terrain of the creosote scrublands, trying to find his way back to his trailer. Prickly pear, ocotillo, yucca, and candlewood scratched at the knees of his worn blue jeans, the elbows of his button-up work shirt. Sick from the heat, crazed with thirst, yet somehow still alive, J.B. sucked on a pebble and yelled obscenities at the porcelain sickle of the moon. In his stupor he blamed it for the father he never knew as a child, for the women who never accepted his love in adulthood, for the whiskey that ruined his career as a boxer.

On the morning of the third day, the boiling eye of the sun banished the moon from the sky. Under this gaze J.B. lay crushed in the dirt by the heat. As his skin blistered in the sun, his thoughts drifted back to the slow Sunday mornings of his childhood. In his head he saw himself sitting in the front pew of St. Luke's in El Paso, his tired head resting against his mother's warm shoulder. With these thoughts in mind, J.B. looked up and begged God to save his life. It was what his mother would have wanted him to do.

While a pair of buzzards swam lazy circles in the blue sky above, J.B. saw a black dot emerge from the molten disk of the sun. For the next few minutes he shaded his eyes with his sunburned hand and watched the dot float gracefully to the ground, like a vulture riding the thermals. By the time the thing's feet crunched in the rocky earth before him, J.B. couldn't stop himself from croaking out a dry, painful laugh. He did this because the thing standing in front of him was no one other than Foreman Douglas, his chickenshit of a boss he'd wanted to fight so badly three days ago.

"Now you goddamn show up," J.B. croaked, his voice shredded and thin, barely audible over the whirl of the wind. "When I'm half dead and caint hardly stand."

"You asked, and I appeared," Foreman Douglas said. "Did you not beg me to save your life?"

"That was a private conversation between me and God," J.B. said. "I didn't ask you for shit. Except for maybe a chance to break your jaw with a right cross."

Foreman Douglas smiled and spread his arms in a gesture of welcome.

"You may very well get the chance. But how do you know I'm not the one you refer to as God? How do you know I'm not here to save your life?"

J.B. pressed his palms into the warm earth and pushed himself into a sit. For a full minute he tried to figure out if the man standing before him really was God, or if he was just a hallucination of his thirst-crazed mind. After a while J.B. realized it didn't matter either way, because from the smug grin on the man's face, J.B. could see he wasn't here to help.

"Well, the way I figure," J.B. said, his voice rasping painfully, "it don't matter who you are, because one look at your face tells me you ain't my friend. So I'd appreciate it if you'd buzz off and let me die in peace. But if the only reason you're here is to watch me burn and twitch under your little magnifying glass, then I might have something to say about that, if you catch my meaning."

The foreman smiled again and nodded.

"Splendid. One last fight before you fall stone-dead in the dirt. Even on the brink of death, you never change. You are such a fascinatingly irrational man."

"Yeah, well, I tend to get a bit ornery when a pompous ass with a shit-eating grin tries to make a fool out of me for his own amusement."

"I see," Foreman Douglas said. "I knew this form would

awaken your thirst for violence, but I didn't expect such open hostility. In the past you've always been much more skilled at concealing your anger. You never cease to surprise me, Jonathan."

"You don't get to call me that," J.B. said, his throat a pipe of burning coals. "There's only one person on this earth who has permission to call me that, and she's long dead."

"Ah yes. Your dear mother Masie. Bless her foolish little heart," Foreman Douglas said. He bowed his head and crossed himself, but his smug grin remained, which poisoned the gesture with an air of mockery. "All that talk about faith, and yet she refused to believe that her beloved Marlboro Reds would ever do her any harm. No wonder you're so stubborn." He stepped forward and offered J.B. a hand. "Shall we begin?"

J.B. turned his head to the side and tried to spit, but nothing came out. His lips were scorched and split, and his tongue lay dry and swollen in his mouth. Ignoring the foreman's hand, J.B. put on a performance of exaggerated weakness and scrabbled to his feet on his own. As one of the skinniest kids in school while growing up, this had always been J.B.'s most effective strategy for winning fights: play up your own weakness, watch them get overconfident, and then smash them with all you've got. And just like all the other times, the trick worked once again: Foreman Douglas's shoulders relaxed; his hands dropped to his waist; his head cocked to the side in amusement. An instant later, J.B. snapped a quick left jab which caught Foreman Douglas square in the nose. As the foreman stumbled backward in surprise, J.B. juked with his left shoulder and darted forward a half step and let fly a flurry of two right jabs, a left cross, three solid blows to the body, and a right uppercut that grazed the tip of his opponent's exposed chin.

Following this attack, J.B.'s legs collapsed beneath him. His body trembled and quaked with exhaustion. His heart hammered in his ears. With an aching hand pressed to the ground, he gulped huge dry breaths of desert air. No longer exaggerating his weakness, J.B. looked up at his opponent. Though it was clear his attack had done no damage, Foreman Douglas's cocky smile had finally disappeared. Instead the man glowered at J.B. with wrath and anger.

Foreman Douglas raised his arm to the sky and shouted a series of words in an alien language J.B. had never heard before. Sensing retribution, J.B. corralled his remaining strength, leaped forward, and clamped his arms around Foreman Douglas's flabby beer gut. An instant later, a crackling branch of purple lightning sliced the sky in two.

For the next few minutes, the jagged knuckles of the mountains lay hidden behind a thick haze of smoke and dust. Soon the haze cleared and Foreman Douglas pushed J.B.'s dead body aside and clambered to his feet. With his hair disintegrated and his clothes burned to dust, the foreman stood naked in the hard morning sunlight, his pink skin glazed with dirt and ash. To his right, small orange flames slowly devoured a creosote bush. Aside from the quiet crackle of these flames and the screech of a distant buzzard, the land lay quiet, still, and peaceful.

The foreman looked down at J.B.'s lightning-charred body. Thin strings of gray smoke leaked from his eyes, his nostrils, the open tops of his partially-melted boots.

"Impressive. I didn't think you had such courage and ingenuity in you, Jonathan. Based on this showing, I think you've earned yourself another chance. Next time, I hope you'll find a way to put your skills to better use," Foreman Douglas said. He kneeled in the dirt and kissed J.B.'s blackened forehead. By the time he stood up, J.B.'s body was gone. "Until we meet again, son, I'll be waiting for you here. I hope to see you soon."

In the Garden of Earthly Delights

Me and Kyoko were driving home from a nice pasta dinner at
our old friend Gretchen's house when God appeared in the back
seat of our car and granted Kyoko one wish for saving Gretchen's
life all those years ago at Action Park.

"So what's your wish, Kyoko?" God said, after Kyoko
pulled over onto the side of the road and thought for a few
minutes.

"Hmmm . . ." Kyoko said, craning her head to the side
and looking up at the roof of the car. A black SUV whooshed
past. Blue headlights flashed harshly in the rear-view mirror. A
blast of rushing air sent our car rocking. Resting her hands in her
lap, Kyoko looked over at me and grinned.

"I wish for me and Nick to be transported into the
world of Hieronymus Bosch's Garden of Earthly Delights."

"An interesting choice," God said, nodding. "I hope it
helps you find what you're looking for." Then he snapped his
fingers and disappeared.

"Who's Hieronymus Bosch?" I said to Kyoko. "And
what's the Garden of Earthly Delights?"

"It's a three-panel painting from—oh shit," Kyoko said,
her hand rising to her mouth. "I forgot to tell him which panel to
put us in."

"Does that matter?" I said. "What kind of painting is
it?"

"Eh, I think it'll be fine. Since he's God, I'm sure he
knows which panel I was talking about," Kyoko said, resting her
hand on my thigh. I shuddered a little at her touch. My body
tensed with anxiety. "Don't worry. You're going to love it. It's
exactly what we need to get the old spark back."

I forced a smile onto my face and nodded. Ever since
me and Kyoko got back together three months ago, things had
been going pretty good. She had started wearing her wedding ring
again, and we were communicating better than ever before. The
only thing that hadn't come back yet was the sex. Back when we
were together the first time, sex was the only way Kyoko knew
how to open up and to let me into the secret world of her inner
life. But now that we were older, wiser, and better at expressing
ourselves, our communication wasn't as dependent on physical

intimacy. Because of that, we'd only slept together once in the past three months. That scared me. Kyoko was starting to get bored, and my anxiety was creating some very embarrassing performance issues which only exacerbated the problem. And that wasn't good, because I knew how quickly Kyoko could change her mind again and leave me behind without another thought.

Feeling the warmth of her hand on my thigh, I took a deep breath and tried to relax my body. Then I rested my hand on top of hers and squeezed.

"Okay," I said. "Let's try it."

#

Moments later we found ourselves lying naked on our backs in a lush meadow of green grass, tall trees, and small ponds of clear water. Fantastical animals that only exist in dreams grazed all around us, while God, looking youthful and dapper in a set of silky pink robes, stood to our left. A man and a woman were with him, but all three were too distracted by their own business to notice our presence. In the pond near our feet, a fish with gleaming silver scales and white-feathered wings stared up at us with eyes like wet black marbles. A strange creature with the head of a horse, the long horn of a narwhal, and the thick body of a manatee swam circles around the winged fish. At the far end of the pool, a small man wearing the costume of a duck-billed platypus read a heavy book while floating in the water.

"Isn't it beautiful?" God said to us from behind.

"It really is," Kyoko said, glancing up at the oak and cherry trees swaying slowly in the breeze. She grabbed my hand and started leading me toward the tree line to the east. While we walked, she leaned in close and whispered in my ear. "We're in the first panel of the painting right now, but we want to be in the second. I think it's this way. Follow me."

The sounds of human voices, chirping animals, and sloshing water grew louder as we approached the tree line.

"Don't do it, Kyoko," God said, his voice suddenly sharp and paternal. "That's a place of sin. And you know exactly where it leads. Everything you need is right here."

Kyoko squeezed my hand and nodded.

Trust me, she mouthed.

I nodded and squeezed her hand in agreement.

"Thanks," Kyoko said to God, "but I think we'll be okay. It's not like we're going to steal anything or kill anyone or . . ." she turned to me and shrugged. "What were the other commandments again?"

"I don't remember," I said, looking at her with worry. "But are you sure you want to antagonize him like this? Shouldn't we listen to what he says?"

"Don't worry about it," she said, turning sideways and squeezing through the narrow gap between the two gnarled oak trees before us. "We're good people. We earned this. As long as we don't break any of his commandments, we don't have to worry about the third panel of the painting. Now give me your hand."

She stuck her hand through the gap in the trees.

"Wait, what happens in the third panel?" I said.

"An apocalypse of death, torture, and mutilation rains down upon the sinners of the earth," she said. "But you're going to forget all about that when you see what's over here in the second panel. Please trust me, Nick. We need this. I wouldn't have wished for it if the risk outweighed the reward."

I looked at Kyoko's hand and then back up to her brown eyes visible through the gap in the trees. I drew a deep breath and grabbed her hand.

"Disappointing," God said, in a quiet voice. "I'm very disappointed in both of you."

Kyoko ignored him and gave me a wide smile as she pulled me through the gap in the trees and led me into the second panel of the painting.

#

The second panel was even more beautiful than the first. Just past the tree line, the ground sloped downward and we waded into a shallow lake. The lake sat at the edge of a pastoral paradise of rolling grassy fields, surreal stone architecture, and spotless blue sky. In the center of the lake, a group of naked men and women kissed and played games alongside a wild duck as big as a grizzly bear. To our left, a trio of women took greedy bites out of a basketball- sized blackberry dangling from the beak of an enormous finch. On the right, a pair of lovers peered out from inside a massive hollow apple floating on the surface of the water, while a stray leg from a different couple having sex behind them burst through the hardened skin of the apple. In a nearby field, dozens of naked men and women frolicked blissfully among a playground of gigantic fruit pods.

As we waded farther into the lake, the sounds of contented laughter, splashing water, and beautiful birdsongs filled the warm air around us.

"This place is unbelievable," I said, noticing a warm pink flush in Kyoko's cheeks.

"Now you know why I wished for this," she said, licking her lips and giving me The Look. "If this doesn't reignite the old spark between us, nothing will."

My heart thudded heavily in my chest. My palms slicked wet with anxious sweat. My throat tightened at the thought of disappointing her again.

"So what do you want to do first?" I said.

Kyoko wrapped her arm around my waist and pointed at a ring of people crowded around a man standing in the grass on the other side of the lake. Pairs of shiny red cherries as big as billiard balls sat atop of a few of the onlookers' heads, while the man in the center of the crowd drank from a shimmering jug shaped like the thorax of a large insect. Once the man was done drinking, he belched loudly, handed the jug to one of the members of the crowd, and passionately kissed the man to his right.

"Let's see what's going on over there," Kyoko said. She tugged me over to the crowd of people and wormed through the ring of bodies to the center. For five minutes I stood next to her and watched as she yelled into the cacophonous chatter of the crowd and asked for a chance to drink from the shimmering jug. No one answered her or even acknowledged our presence.

Instead, they laughed and kissed and passed the jug back and forth between themselves. After another five minutes of being ignored, Kyoko snatched the jug from the hands of the woman standing next to us. The woman yelped in surprise; the crowd yelled angry admonishments.

Ignoring these, Kyoko tucked the jug under her arm, forced her way through the crowd, and started running toward a large lake on the other side of the field. Punches and kicks rained down on me as I clawed my way through the crowd to follow

Kyoko. Once I caught up to her, I grabbed her hand and we ran, our bare feet thumping against the soft dirt beneath the grass. We ran until we reached the edge of the large lake northeast of where we entered this panel of the painting. When we turned around and looked behind us, we saw that the crowd had given up the chase after a few seconds.

Kyoko grinned at me and leaned the jug back and drank. Clear, foamy liquid dribbled from the corners of her mouth.

"Whoa, that's really good," she said, handing the jug to me. "You have to try this. It reminds me of watermelon juice, but a little bit thicker. And I think I taste some vanilla in there too."

I took a long swig from the jug, my heart still beating hard from the run. Kyoko was right, the liquid was delicious. It had the clean, sweet taste of pulp-free watermelon juice, and the rich, creamy finish of a vanilla milkshake.

"Oh wow, yeah, that's great," I said, handing the jug back to her. But she wasn't interested in it anymore. Instead, she dropped it on the ground, pressed her warm body against mine, and started kissing me. I pulled back and tried to still my trembling fingers. "Do you think we could go somewhere more private, at least?"

Kyoko stared at me for a long moment and sighed. Then she looked around the open field and saw a man carrying a giant mussel shell on his back. Bending down and picking up the shimmering jug of exotic juice, Kyoko called out to the man and waved him over. After negotiating with the man for a few minutes, she traded the shimmering jug for the giant mussel shell.

The man and I placed the shell onto the surface of the nearby lake and pried it open. Kyoko slithered inside first; I followed. With the shimmering jug clutched in his left hand, the man waved to us, let the shell snap shut, and pushed us out toward the center of the lake.

It was hot and slippery inside the shell. Soft pink flesh lined the walls and ceiling. Despite the stuffiness, we had more than enough room to lay down and stretch our legs to their full length. Noticing this, Kyoko climbed on top of me and mashed her lips against mine. But after a minute of making out, she pulled away and peeled a sheet of sweat-soaked hair off her forehead.

"Jesus Christ, it's so fucking hot in here," she said,

pressing her palms against the top half of the mussel shell. Fat droplets of sweat dripped from the points of her elbows. "I'm sorry, Nick, but we have to open this shell. I feel like I'm going to suffocate in here."

I sat up and grabbed her wrists.

"Please don't," I said, my voice warbling with anxiety. "If I can't . . . I don't want them to see me disappoint you like that."

Kyoko leaned forward, held my face in her hands, and looked at me for a long time. Her cheeks flushed a deep pink. Her gold brown eyes glinted like crystalized amber.

"You have to forget about the past," she said. "Everything that happened before this doesn't matter anymore. We're here, together, right now. And there's nowhere else I'd rather be. He gave *me* the wish, not you. So if I wanted something else, or someone else, I would've wished for that. But I didn't. Because I want you. And I know you always used to tell me that I was so closed off and that I never let anyone into my world, but that's not the case anymore. It took a hell of a lot of pain and hard work for me to get to this point, but I made it. Now it's your turn. Because in order for things to work out between us this time, you have to open up to *me*. And the world. You have to let us in. And I know it's scary, because the only time people can truly hurt you is when you let them in. But you have to, Nick. You have to let me in, or else we're never going to get past this."

I slurped a deep breath and tried to slow the frantic thudding of my heart.

"But I don't even—how do I do that?"

Kyoko smiled and flicked a trembling droplet of sweat from her chin.

"Opening this shell would be a good start."

"Okay," I said with a sharp exhale. "You can open it."

She shook her head.

"No. You have to do it. That's the only way it's going to work."

I stared at her for a long moment and then nodded.

"Okay, roll over," I said, grabbing her by the ribs and sliding her under me. "This really must be an alternate reality if you're lecturing me about emotional vulnerability."

"Didn't see that coming, did you?" she said with a

laugh.

"No, I did not," I said, pressing my hands against the slippery pink flesh above my head.

After an initial resistance, the top half of the shell snapped off at the connection point behind Kyoko's head and splashed into the lake. Cool spring air washed over our sweat-drenched bodies. The sounds of laughing people and chirping birds filled our ears once again. Before I could enjoy any more of the beautiful scenery, Kyoko rolled on top of me and kissed me passionately. Moments later, we heard a familiar voice.

"I'm glad to see you two are having fun," God said, from above. "But all sinners must face judgement sooner or later. And I'm afraid that time is now."

"Just ignore him," Kyoko said, breaking away from me for a moment, her breath rolling warm and heavy past my ear. "He can't touch us. We didn't do anything wrong."

"Thou shalt not steal," God said.

"But we didn't steal this shell, we traded for it with the . . . oh," Kyoko said.

"Yes," God said. "And since you stole that juice, it's time for you to experience the third panel of the painting."

Kyoko grabbed my hand and looked up at God, who now wore a set of royal blue robes similar to the color of the sky.

"Wait, please, what if we repent for our sins and ask for forgiveness?" She said, squeezing my hand in fear. "Could you find it in your heart to spare us from the third panel?"

God stared down at us with a blank expression. Then, slowly, the corners of his lips curled into a small, satisfied smile. His eyes smoldered like the embers of a dying fire. Heavy black storm clouds choked the blue sky behind him.

"No," he said, in a quiet voice. "Sinners like you don't get a second chance."

#

The third panel of the painting was more terrifying than I had imagined. Me and Kyoko awoke on a barren beach peppered with rolling dunes of hot sand, spiny tufts of dry scrub grass, and sharp shards of volcanic glass. All around us naked men and women screamed in pain as they received punishment for their earthly sins. On the left, a pair of musicians hung impaled on the gleaming steel strings of a giant harp as tall as a two story house. To our right, a blindfolded gambling addict hunched behind an overturned card table while a wolf in human clothes stabbed him in the neck with a longsword. In the distance, roaring fires and violent conflicts ravaged the ruins of a vast, ancient city squatting on the bank of a meandering river. Overhead, huge knives clutched between pairs of floating, disembodied ears patrolled the beach like prison guards.

Scrabbling to our feet, me and Kyoko saw that God had placed us in the middle of a long line of naked sinners slowly walking toward a demonic figure sitting atop a wooden throne. The throne stood over twenty feet tall and hovered above a circular hole in the ground ringed with the orange glow of liquid magma. The demon sitting atop the throne had the head of a sparrow and the body of a man, and he wore a set of royal blue robes nearly identical to those God had been wearing just before he banished us into this panel of the painting. A black, cast-iron kettle rested on top of the demon's head in the place of a crown, and a pair of yellow clay pots sheathed his stubby feet like crude, breakable shoes.

"Jesus Christ," I said, shifting my weight to the left and right to alleviate the burning pain in my feet.

"I know," Kyoko said. Then she pointed at the demon sitting on the throne. "Just wait till you see what's waiting for us up ahead."

I grabbed Kyoko's hand and looked to the front of the line of sinners. Each time a new sinner reached the foot of the demon's throne, the floating ears skewered them through the chest with their knives and presented them to the demon for judgement. But the sinner's offense didn't seem to matter, because in each case the punishment was the same: the demon grabbed the sinner with his powerful hands, swallowed the screaming victim whole, and shat them out into the glowing hole to hell beneath the throne, where they disappeared in a flash of orange light and a small plume of black smoke.

"This is crazy," I whispered into Kyoko's ear. "We have to get out of here."

She nodded in agreement, and we both started looking for a way to escape.

After a minute of scanning the landscape, Kyoko squeezed my hand and gestured with her head in the direction of the demon wearing the blue robes.

"The wall behind his throne," she whispered. "Look at it. It's not connected to a building or any other type of structure. It just goes on into infinity in every direction, all the way up into the sky and through the clouds. I think that's the end of the painting. If we can break through that, we might be able to get out of here for good."

I looked at the wall. She was right. It extended all the way to the burning city beside the river and beyond. But with the floating ears preventing any escape from the line of sinners, there was only one direction for us to go: straight toward the demon on the throne.

"Yeah, that's got to be the edge of the painting," I whispered back to Kyoko. "But how can we—"

Just then the woman in line behind us tapped me on the shoulder. "You can't get away by yourselves, if that's what you're thinking," the woman said. An Ibanez electric guitar hung from the woman's left shoulder; a six-inch hole in her chest stared at me like a cat's vertical pupil; a Yamaha electric guitar amp sat fused to her back like a sixty- pound tumor. Ear piercing feedback squealed from the amp each time she moved her body and jostled the strings of her guitar. "You're going to need someone to distract the ears while you get away."

I looked at Kyoko and then back to the woman.

"You would do that for us?" I said.

"Sure," she said, playing a quick metal riff on her guitar. In an instant the ears swarmed around her and started slicing her arms with their knives until she stopped playing. "Alright, alright, fuckers, I'm done!" she said to the floating ears. Dropping her bloody arms to her sides, she looked back at me and Kyoko. "As you can see, I'd do anything to get out of this shithole. I just want to get back to playing with my band and hanging out with my girlfriend, Heather. Things were finally going good in my life when those squid alien assholes showed up and ruined everything."

"I'm sorry to hear that," Kyoko said to the woman. "But thanks for your help. Once you have the ears distracted, we'll make a break for the wall and punch through. Then we'll hold off the ears while you run to the wall. Sound good?"

Kyoko looked at me and then back to the woman. We both nodded.

"Sorry to rain on your parade there folks, but your little plan just ain't gonna work," said the man standing in line in front of us. Neon purple scars like the branches of a fern curled down the entire length of the man's body, all the way to the backs of his heels. He stood half a head shorter than both me and Kyoko, and he couldn't have weighed more than a hundred and twenty pounds, but hard disks of muscle rippled beneath his scarred skin with each relaxed breath. "You caint do nothing in this place without taking care a that chickenshit right up there with the pot on his head," the man said, flicking his chin at the demon sitting on the throne. "He runs the show round these parts, and if he sees anyone making a break for that wall, all he's gotta do is say a couple a special words and your ass is grass. Believe me, I know." The man pointed at the scars on his back with a deformed hand.

Kyoko leaned forward and studied the man's back.

"The demon up there gave you these scars?" Kyoko said.

"Yes ma'am," the man said. "Me and that chickenshit up there were having it out in the west Texas desert when he started saying these weird-ass words in some other language I never heard before. A few seconds later I woke up here, looking like this."

Kyoko glanced at me and then back to the scars on the man's body.

"These are Lichtenberg figures," she said. "They show up when a person gets struck by lightning."

"So that's how that little shit k.o.'d me," The man said. "Once a cheater, always a cheater."

The man shook his head and scoffed. Then he held one of his oddly-shaped hands over his mouth and drank the amber liquid pouring from the hardened digit that used to be his thumb. Studying his deformed hands for the first time, I saw that all his fingers were gone, and that both of his hands had been molded into flesh-covered whiskey bottles. But this divine punishment didn't seem to bother the man in the least.

"Would you be willing to challenge him to a rematch in order to distract him while we get away?" Kyoko said to the man.

"Darlin, there ain't nothing I'd rather do right about now," the man said, wiping his mouth with the back of his wrist. "You just tell me when, and I'll march right up to the front a this line and challenge him to a rematch in front a all these fine folks. I'll even let him keep his cute little birdie mask on."

"Okay good, so we're set," Kyoko said, turning back to me and the guitar woman. "Once our friend here has the demon distracted, you'll start playing your guitar to get the attention of the ears. Then, when they swarm you, me and Nick will make a break for the wall. Once we've punched through the wall, you'll throw away your guitar and meet up with us. Sound good?"

The guitar woman nodded, but I craned my head to the side and looked at Kyoko.

"Wait, how are we going to break through the wall? We don't have anything to—" I said.

"Please, Nick," Kyoko said, squeezing my hand. "You have to trust me."

"But I—"

"Please. Just trust me."

I looked at her for a long moment. My heart smashed in my ears. My mouth went dry. Slowly, her lips curled into a small smile. Feeling some of my anxiety dissolve away, I nodded.

"Okay," I said. "I trust you."

Kyoko squeezed my hand and tapped the scarred man on the shoulder. "We're all set," she whispered into his ear. "Whenever you're ready."

The scarred man nodded and bounced on his toes and smacked his whiskey-bottle hands together a few times. After a sharp exhale and a crackling stretch of his neck, he started pushing his way to the front of the line.

"Pardon me, coming through, out of the way, very important business here, folks," he said, as he shoved naked sinners out of his way.

When he reached the foot of the wooden throne, he looked up and pointed his deformed hand at the demon wearing the blue robes.

"I want a rematch," the scarred man said, as the ears swarmed around him. "You and me. One on one. Right here. And I'll even let you wear your cute little birdie mask so you don't get embarrassed in front a all these fine folks when I kick your ass."

Just before the ears skewered the scarred man through the chest, the demon held up a hand and stopped them.

"After all the chances I've given you, Jonathan, this is

how you repay me? With more anger and threats of violence? Haven't we done this enough?"

Jonathan turned his head to the side and spat.

"Well, mama always said I'm as stubborn as a one-eyed donkey, so I reckon one more time ought to cover it."

The demon shook his head and sighed.

"Disappointing," he said, rising from the throne and floating to the ground. Moments after the clay pots on his feet touched the sand, he slipped off his blue robes. Then he slid the cast-iron kettle off his head and tossed it behind his throne, where it smacked against the boundary wall with a hard thunk. Grabbing his beak with his right hand, he pulled off the sparrow mask.

Me and Kyoko watched this scene from our vantage point in the line of sinners. When Kyoko saw that it had been God wearing the sparrow mask the entire time, she shook her head in disgust.

"Goddamnit," she said. "I knew it was him. This is very bad. Our new friend there doesn't stand a chance."

"What are we going to do?" I said to her.

"Stick to the plan," she said to me with a shrug. "There's nothing else we can do at this point." She turned to the guitar woman. "Get ready. Once they start fighting, play as loud and fast as you can."

The guitar woman nodded and took a few steps back. She rested her bloody hands on her guitar and waited. Me and Kyoko looked back at Jonathan and God.

God let go of the sparrow mask and crossed his arms behind his back. Just before the mask touched the ground, Jonathan darted forward and blanketed God with a pair of right jabs, a left cross to the chin, a right hook to the body, three right jabs to the side of the head, and a left cross to the crown of a perfect cheekbone. Though each punch connected with a solid, thumping impact, the blows had no effect. They seemed to smack against God's body harmlessly, like raindrops pinging against the windshield of a car.

Jonathan danced backward and held his whiskey-bottle fists in front of his face in anticipation of God's first attack. But God kept his hands behind his back and his eyes fixed on Jonathan. Sensing her opportunity, the guitar woman strummed a deafening chord that quickly devolved into a sludgy, chugging, death-metal riff. Gradually increasing the tempo and intensity of her playing, the guitar woman swirled her frizzy blonde hair and thrashed her body with wild abandon. This sudden cacophony of sound and motion sent the floating ears whirling in disoriented, drunken circles; two pairs of ears hovering above Jonathan's head crashed into each other and fell to the ground in a mess of impaled cartilage and blood-slicked steel. The remaining four pairs left Jonathan and God behind and started swarming the guitar woman.

Kyoko squeezed my hand and we ran toward the boundary wall. Shards of volcanic glass sliced the aching soles of my feet. Fiery sand scoured the open cuts on my heels. Smoke-saturated air shredded my dry throat. But I clutched Kyoko's hand and kept going.

We reached the border wall in less than a minute. Circling behind the wooden throne, I looked to Kyoko.

"What do we do now?" I said, gulping serrated breaths, my bloody feet roaring in pain.

Kyoko fell to her knees and started digging through the sand.

"Find something to break through the wall," she said. "There's got to be a rock or one of these pieces of obsidian we can use."

Clawing at the sand, I found rough tufts of scrub grass and more shards of volcanic glass, but nothing that could break through the wall. Each shard of volcanic glass was too sharp to get a firm grip.

Moments later, Kyoko yelled to me.

"Nick, over here, help me with this," she said, pulling at the handle of the cast-iron kettle God had been wearing as a crown while pretending to be the demon prince. "It's too heavy for me. Try to hit it against the wall."

I scrabbled over to her and tried to lift the kettle. A wet groan tumbled from my throat as I strained, but I could only lift it two or three feet off the ground before my arms and shoulders burned with crackling pain.

I dropped the kettle on the ground and rubbed my sweaty hands in the sand.

"It's too heavy," I said. I pointed to the left side of the kettle's circular handle. "You take that end and we'll swing it together. This thing has got to have enough weight to break through the wall."

Kyoko nodded at me and grabbed the other end of the kettle. Before I gave her the signal to lift, I took a quick look around. Jonathan darted around the glowing hole to hell and jabbed at God with his whiskey-bottle hands. The guitar woman fought off the ears with the percussive punch of a galloping riff and the swinging headstock of her Ibanez guitar. Satisfied that the plan was working, I looked back to Kyoko and counted down from three. On zero we lifted the kettle out of the sand and started smacking it against the wall.

The wooden wall cracked with each impact of the kettle. Forked rivulets of cloudy sweat scudded down my forehead. Gritty smears of sand-caked blood covered my throbbing hands.

After two frantic minutes of exertion, we punched through the wall and cleared out a hole just big enough for a single person to squeeze through. Thrusting my head through the hole, I smelled cool, crisp autumn air: the same air me and Kyoko had walked out into after our dinner at Gretchen's house. But before I could step out of the way and usher Kyoko through the hole, I heard God's voice behind us.

"Don't try it, Nick," he said, absorbing three of Jonathan's punches directly to his chin. "It's not going to work. Kyoko wished for this, so you two are stuck here with me for good."

Just then Jonathan circled around behind God, leaped over the glowing hole to hell, and wrapped his arms around God's neck.

"Go on!" Jonathan said. "Get outta here before he can call down his lightning!"

I nodded at Jonathan and threw a shard of volcanic glass at the guitar woman's feet to get her attention. Moments later she looked up from her headbanging and nodded. She slid her guitar off her shoulder and swung it like an ax at the swarming ears. With a satisfying crunch, the electric-blue Ibanez connected with a pair of the floating ears and sent them flying into the nearby river. A few of the naked sinners clapped and broke out into cheers. Then the guitar woman dropped her guitar on the ground and ran in our direction.

I turned back to Kyoko and started ushering her through the hole in the wall. Before she could squeeze through,

God shouted a wrathful command in a strange language I'd never heard before. But Jonathan wrenched God's head backward and choked off the last few words of this command. In retaliation, God ground his elbow into Jonathan's stomach, and the two of them teetered off balance toward the hole to hell underneath God's throne. Hearing God's command, me, Kyoko, and the guitar woman dropped to the ground and took cover.

A blinding purple light flashed around us. A crackling roar of thunder crashed overhead. After a few moments of eerie stillness, I opened my eyes and checked on Kyoko and the guitar woman. None of us were harmed. Turning around, I saw Jonathan and God teetering closer to the glowing orange hole underneath God's burning throne.

"Nice shot, deadeye, but it looks like your aim was a little bit off this time," Jonathan said to God. "You gone and torched your fancy-pants toilet throne instead a me. And now you and I are goin for a little swim together."

Jonathan gave us a wide grin as he fell backward into hell and took God along for the ride.

Seconds after Jonathan and God disappeared, the remaining ears swarmed the three of us and started slashing at us with their knives. I tossed shards of volcanic glass at the ears while Kyoko used another shard to cut the Yamaha amp off the guitar woman's back. Once the woman was free from her divine punishment, Kyoko helped her through the hole in the boundary wall. Kyoko followed. Then, just before the remaining ears executed a three-pronged pincer attack on me, I grabbed Kyoko's out-thrust arm and slipped through the narrow hole in the wall.

#

Moments later, the three of us tumbled naked into the backseat of Kyoko's Honda sedan, which was still sitting on the side of Grove Street right where we had left it. After a minute of awkward untangling, me and Kyoko climbed into the front seats and gave the guitar woman one of the blankets Kyoko kept in the backseat for emergencies.

With the guitar woman taken care of, Kyoko handed me the other emergency blanket and a package of disinfectant wipes from the glove compartment. While I tended to my bloody feet and hands, Kyoko turned the key, which was still in the ignition, and started the car. She glanced at me and then at the guitar woman in the back seat.

"So, hospital?"

"We should probably stop over at your place and get some clothes first," I said to Kyoko.

"That's a good idea," the guitar woman said. "I personally don't give a shit either way, but I don't want the nurses to think you two kidnapped me or something. This hole in my chest will be pretty hard for anyone to explain. I'm not really looking forward to it."

"Oh yeah, I forgot about that," I said. "What happened to you? How did you get that?"

"It's a long story," the guitar woman said. "I'll tell you about it some other time."

"Okay," Kyoko said. "But does it hurt? Are you going to be okay?"

The guitar woman opened the blanket and looked down at her chest. With the guitar amp gone from her back, her wound was now a six-inch, see-through vertical slit near the center of her torso. The flesh around the wound gleamed with the shiny, metallic luster of polished gold, and the edges of the wound were as sharp and precise as those of a cut diamond.

"No, it doesn't hurt at all," she said, prodding curiously at the wound. "I'm not sure if that's good or bad, but right now I feel fine."

She closed the blanket and looked up at us and shrugged.

"I'm up for whatever," she said. "Just as long as I get to call my girlfriend before we do anything."

"Sounds good to me," Kyoko said, turning around and shifting the car into drive. She pulled out onto the road and pressed her bare foot to the gas. "We'll stop at my house for some clothes, and then it's off to the hospital."

#

We pulled into Kyoko's driveway ten minutes later. Just before she opened her door to get out, I rested my hand on her leg and looked at her. She nodded at me and spun around in her seat and handed the keys to the guitar woman.

"We're going to stay here and talk for a minute, but you can go inside and call your girlfriend if you want," Kyoko said to the guitar woman. "The phone is hanging on the wall in the kitchen."

The guitar woman nodded in thanks, wrapped the blanket around her shoulders, and climbed out of the car. Once she disappeared inside the house, I turned to Kyoko and flashed a tired smile.

"I have a question," I said.

"Just one?" She said, grinning.

"One important one," I said. "If you didn't find that kettle behind the demon's throne, what did you think we were going to use to break through the wall? What was your plan there?"

Kyoko laughed and shook her head.

"I didn't have a plan. But I believed that the two of us working together would find a way to get through it. And we did."

"That's it?"

"Yeah. But it wouldn't have worked unless both of us took that chance together. And that's what this is all about," she said, placing her hand on top of mine.

"Yeah," I said, looking to the front door of Kyoko's house, which the guitar woman had left wide open. "You're right."

Kyoko smiled at me and followed my gaze. When she saw the open door, her smile disappeared.

"See, this is exactly why no one should have the infinite powers of a god. Because if it was up to me right now, I'd banish her right back to hell just for leaving the door—" Kyoko started to say, when I leaned over the center column and kissed her.

She rested her hand on my leg and kissed me back. A few seconds later, she broke away.

"What if she comes out and catches us?" Kyoko said.

I gave her The Look and climbed into the back seat.

"Who cares?" I said, and offered her my hand.

A Note About the Type

The text of this book was set in C. x Paradisi Gothic, a typeface designed by Mary Harrington (1939–2015), a poet, swimmer, graphic designer, and pen-and-ink artist. In addition to these pursuits, Ms. Harrington was also the mother of the author of this note. (The author of this note and the author of the book that preceded it are one and the same.) C. x Paradisi Gothic is a neo-grotesque sans-serif typeface, and like the woman who created it, it concedes no space to unnecessary decorations and adornments. Sleek, clean lines and neutral, uncluttered letterforms are the order of the day. The typeface takes its name from the taxonomic classification of the pink grapefruit, the citrus fruit whose juice Ms. Harrington would drink each morning after completing her forty minute swim at the Grove Street Recreation Center near her home in Topine, NY. Ms. Harrington maintained this routine every day for over forty years, including her final day on this planet, December 6, 2015.

On that day, the author of this note accompanied Ms. Harrington to the Grove Street Recreation Center. Once there, the author entered the pool and attempted to keep pace with her seventy-six-year-old senior for the duration of the forty minute session. She failed. (Her attempt to drink an entire glass of pink grapefruit juice following this workout was also met with failure.) Later that day, while sipping a glass of Pinot Noir and pressing an ice pack to a shoulder already sore from the morning's swim, the author watched Ms. Harrington sketch what would be her final artwork: a pen-and-ink still life of a bowl of mixed fruit. Included in this bowl, alongside a pair of spotted bananas, a trio of furry peaches, and a bunch of plump cherries, was, as expected, a pink grapefruit.

The next morning the author found Ms. Harrington on her back in bed. Her body was cold and unmoving, her eyes gently closed. In addition to this, Ms. Harrington's lips were crinkled into a curious scowl of frustration, as if death was nothing more than a tiresome inconvenience standing in the way of yet another productive day. For the next hour the author sat with Ms. Harrington in a serene silence, and there the two women reminisced about old times.

At the time of Ms. Harrington's death, her typeface did

not have a name; this issue was easily resolved however, thanks to Ms. Harrington's final artwork and a quick Google search. One month later, the London-based graphic designer Jo Webster converted C. x Paradisi Gothic into digital form.

As of this writing, C. x Paradisi Gothic is available online for free download in a single weight and width: the one you've been staring at for the past one hundred odd pages. If this is not acceptable, you may air your grievance with Ms. Harrington when you see her. If you dare.